Four for Fantasy

FOUR FOR FANTASY

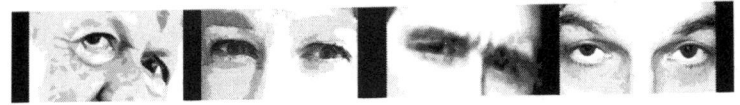

A quartet of fantastical stories collected for World FantasyCon 2013

Brian Aldiss

Joanne Harris

Joe Hill

Richard Christian Matheson

FOUR FOR FANTASY
Copyright © 2013
Brian Aldiss, Joanne Harris,
Joe Hill, Richard Christian Matheson

Edited by Peter Crowther

Published in October 2013 by PS Publishing Ltd. by arrangement with the authors. All rights reserved by the authors. The right of the contributors to be identified as Authors of this Work has been asserted by them in accordance with the Copyright, Designs and Patents Act 1988.

This book is a work of fiction. Names, characters, places and incidents either are products of the authors' imagination or are used fictitiously. Any resemblance to actual events or locales or persons, living or dead, is entirely coincidental.

THE WORM THAT FLIES (Aldiss) Copyright © 1968 by Brian W. Aldiss.
First published in *The Farthest Reaches* edited by Joseph Elder (Pocket Books).
Reprinted by permission of the author and the author's agent.
POP ART (Hill) Copyright © 2001 by Joe Hill. First published in
With Signs & Wonders edited by Daniel M. Jaffe (Invisible Cities Press).
Reprinted by permission of the author and the author's agent.
WAITING FOR GANDALF (Harris) Copyright © 2004 by Joanne Harris.
First published in the author's collection *Jigs and Reels* (Harper).
Reprinted by permission of the author and the author's agent.
CITY OF DREAMS (Matheson) Copyright © 2000 by Richard Christian Matheson.
First published in *Taps and Sighs* edited by Peter Crowther (Subterranean Press).
Reprinted by permission of the author. Author photo courtesy of Diana Mullen.

ISBN 978-1-848636-68-2

Design & Layout by Michael Smith
Printed and bound in England by T.J. International

PS Publishing Ltd Grosvenor House
1 New Road Hornsea, HU18 1PG, England

editor@pspublishing.co.uk
www.pspublishing.co.uk

Contents

Brian Aldiss *The Worm That Flies* 5

Joanne Harris *Waiting for Gandalf* 25

Joe Hill *Pop Art* 43

Richard Christian Matheson *City of Dreams* 65

FOUR FOR FANTASY

Brian Aldiss

The Worm That Flies

Brian Aldiss

The traveller was too absorbed in his reveries to notice when the snow began to fall. He walked slowly, his stiff and elaborate garments, fold over fold, ornament over ornament, standing out from his body like a wizard's tent.

The road along which he travelled had been falling into a great valley, and was increasingly hemmed in by walls of mountain. On several occasions, it had seemed that a way out of these huge accumulations of earth matter could not be found, that the geological puzzle was insoluble, the Chthonian arrangement of discord irresolvable: and then vale and drumlin created between fresh heart and plunged recklessly still deeper into the encompassing upheaval.

The traveller, whose name to his wife was Tapmar and to the rest of the world Argustal, followed this natural harmony incomplete paraesthesia, so close was he in spirit to the atmosphere prevailing here. So strong was this bond, that the freak snowfall merely heightened his rapport.

Though the hour was only midday, the sky became the intense blue-grey of dusk. The Forces were nesting in the sun again, obscuring the light. Consequently, Argustal was scarcely able to detect when the layered and fractured bulwark of rock on his left side, top of which stood unseen perhaps a mile above his head, became patched by artificial means, and he entered the domain of the human company of Or.

As the way made another turn, he saw a wayfarer before him, heading in his direction. It was a great pine, immobile until warmth entered the world again and sap stirred enough in its wooden sinews for it to progress slowly forward once more. He brushed by its green skirts, apologetic but not speaking.

This encounter was sufficient to raise his consciousness above its trance level. His extended mind, which had reached out to embrace the splendid terrestrial discord hereabouts, now shrank to concentrate again on the particularities of his situation, and he saw that he had arrived at Or.

The way bisected itself, unable to choose between two equally unpromising ravines, and Argustal saw a group of humans standing statuesque in the left-hand fork. He went towards them, and stood there silent until they should recognize his presence. Behind him, the wet snow crept into his footprints.

These humans were well advanced into the New Form, even as Argustal had been warned they would be. There were five of them standing here, their great brachial extensions bearing some tender brownish foliage, and one of them attenuated to a height of almost twenty feet. The snow lodged in their branches and in their hair.

Argustal waited for a long span of time, until he judged the afternoon to be well advanced, before growing impatient. Putting his hands to his mouth, he shouted fiercely at them, 'Ho then, Treemen of Or, wake you from your arboreal sleep and converse with me. My name is Argustal to the world, and I travel to my home in far Talembil, where the seas run pink with the spring plankton. I need from you a component for my parapatterner, so rustle yourselves and speak, I beg!'

Now the snow had gone, and a scorching rain driven away its traces. The sun shone again, but its disfigured eye never looked down into the bottom of this ravine. One of the humans shook a branch, scattering water drops all round, and made preparation for speech.

This was a small human, no more than ten feet high, and the old primate from which it had begun to abandon perhaps a couple of million years ago was still in evidence. Among the gnarls and whorls of its naked flesh, its mouth was discernible; this it opened and said, 'We speak to you, Argustal-to-the-world. You are the first ape-human to fare this way in a great time. Thus you are welcome, although you interrupt our search for new ideas.'

'Have you found any new ideas?' Argustal asked, with his customary boldness.

'Indeed. But it is better for our senior to tell you of it, if he so judges good.'

It was by no means clear to Argustal whether he wished to hear what the new idea was, for the Tree-men were known for their deviations into incomprehensibility. But there was a minor furore among the five, as if private winds stirred in their branches, and he settled himself on a boulder, preparing to wait.

His own quest was so important that all impediments to its fulfilment seemed negligible.

Hunger overtook him before the senior spoke. He hunted about and caught slow-galloping grubs under logs, and snatched a brace of tiny fish from the stream, and a handful of nuts from a bush that grew by the stream.

Night fell before the senior spoke. Tall and knotty, his vocal chords were clamped within his gnarled body, and he spoke by curving his branches until his finest twigs, set against his mouth, could be blown through, to give a slender and whispering version of language. The gesture made him seem curiously like a maiden who spoke with her finger cautiously to her lips.

'Indeed we have new idea, O Argustal-to-the-world, though it may be beyond your grasping or our expressing. We have perceived that there is a dimension called time, and from this we have drawn a deduction.'

'We will explain dimensional time simply to you like this. We know that all things have lived so long on Earth that their origins are forgotten. What we can remember carries from that lost-in-the-mist thing up to this present moment; it is the time we inhabit, and we are used to think of it as all the time there is. But we men of Or have reasoned that this is not so.'

'There must be other past times in the lost distances of time,' said Argustal, 'but they are nothing to us because we cannot touch them as we can our own pasts.'

As if this remark had never been, the silvery whisper continued, 'As one mountain looks small when viewed from another, so the things in our past that we remember look small from the present. But suppose we moved back to that past to look at the present! We could not see it—yet we know it exists. And from this we reason that there is still more time in the future, although we cannot see it.'

For a long while, the night was allowed to exist in silence, and then Argustal said, 'Well, I don't see that as being very wonderful reasoning. We know that, if the Forces permit, the sun will shine again tomorrow, don't we?'

The small tree-men who had first spoken, said, 'But 'tomorrow' is expressional time. *We* have discovered that tomorrow exists in dimensional time also. It is real already, as real as yesterday.'

'Holy spirits!' thought Argustal to himself, 'why did I get involved in philosophy?' Aloud he said, 'Tell me of the deduction you have drawn from this.'

Again the silence, until the senior drew together his branches and whispered from a bower of twiggy fingers, 'We have proved that tomorrow is no surprise. It is as unaltered as today or yesterday, merely another yard of the path of time. But we comprehend that things change, don't we? You comprehend that, don't you?'

'Of course. You yourselves are changing, are you not?'

'It is as you say, although we no longer recall what we were before, for that thing is become too small back in time. So: if time is all of the same quality, then it has no change, and thus cannot force change. So: there is another unknown element in the world that forces change!'

Thus in their fragmentary whispers they reintroduced sin into the world.

Because of the darkness, a need for sleep was induced in Argustal. With the senior tree-man's permission, he climbed up into his branches and remained fast asleep until dawn returned to the fragment of sky above the mountains and filtered down to their retreat. Argustal swung to the ground, removed his outer garments, and performed his customary exercises. Then he spoke to the five beings again, telling them of his parapatterner, and asking for certain stones.

Although it was doubtful whether they understood what he was doing, they gave him permission, and he moved round about the area, searching for a necessary stone, his senses blowing into nooks and crannies for it like a breeze.

The ravine was blocked at its far end by a rock fall, but the stream managed to pour through the interstices of the detritus into a yet lower defile. Climbing painfully, Argustal scrambled over the mass of broken rock to find himself in a cold and moist passage, a mere cavity between two great thighs of mountain. Here the light was dim, and the sky could hardly be seen, so far did the rocks overhang on the many shelves of strata overhead. But Argustal scarcely looked up. He followed the steam where it flowed into the rock itself, to vanish forever from human view.

He had been so long at his business, trained himself over so many millennia, that the stones almost spoke to him, and he became more certain than ever that he would find a stone to fit in with his grand design.

It was there. It lay just above the water, the upper part of it polished. When he had prised it out from the surrounding pebbles and gravel, he lifted it and could see that underneath it was slightly jagged, as if a smooth gum grew black teeth. He was surprised, but as he squatted to examine it, he began to see what was necessary to the design his parapatterner was precisely some such roughness. At once, the next step of the design revealed itself, and he saw for the first time the whole thing as it would be in its entirety. The vision disturbed and excited him.

He sat where he was, his blunt fingers round the rough-smooth stone, and for some reason he began to think about his wife Pamitar. Warm feelings of love ran through him, so that he smiled to himself and twitched his brows.

By the time he stood up and climbed out of the defile, he knew much about the new stone. His nose-for-stones sniffed it back to times when it was much larger affair, when it occupied a grand position on a mountain, when it was engulfed in the bowels of the mountain, when it had been cast up and shattered down, when it had been a component of a bed of rock, when that rock had been ooze, when it had been a gentle rain of volcanic sediment, showering through an unbreathable atmosphere and filtering down through warm seas in an early and unknown place.

With a tender respect, he tucked the stone away in a large pocket and scrambled back along the way he had come. He made no farewell to the five of Or. They stood mute together, branch-limbs interlocked, dreaming of the dark sin of change.

Now he made haste for home, travelling first through the borderlands of Old Crotheria and then through the region of Tamia, where there was only mud. Legends had it that Tamia had once known fertility, and that speckled fish had swam in streams between forests; but now mud conquered everything, and the few villages were of baked mud, while the roads were dried mud, the sky was the colour of mud, and the few mud-coloured humans who chose for their own mud-stained reasons to live here had scarcely any antlers growing from their shoulders and seemed about to deliquesce into mud. There wasn't a decent stone anywhere about the place. Argustal met a tree called David-by-the-moat-that-dries which was moving into his own home region. Depressed by the everlasting brownness of Tamia, he begged a ride from it, and climbed into it branches. It was old and gnarled, its branches and roots equally hunched, and it spoke in grating syllables of its few ambitions.

As he listened, taking pains to recall each syllable while he waited long for the next, Argustal saw that David spoke by much the same means as the people of Or had done, stuffing whistling twigs to an orifice in its trunk; but whereas it seemed that the tree-men were losing the use of their vocal chords, it seemed that the man-tree was developing some stringy integuments of its fibres, so that it became a nice problem as to which was inspired by which, which copied which, or whether—for both sides seemed so self-absorbed that this was also a possibility—they had come on a mirror-image of perversity independently.

'Motion is the prime beauty,' said David-by-the-moat-that-dries, and took many degrees of the sun across the muddy sky to say it. 'Motion is in me. There is no motion in the ground. In the ground there is not motion. All that the ground contains is without motion. The ground lies in quiet and to lie in the ground is not to be. Beauty is not in the ground. Beyond the ground is the air. Air and ground make all there is and I would be of the ground and air. I was of the ground and of the air but I will be of the air alone. If there is ground, there is another ground. The leaves fly in the air and my longing goes with them but they are only part of me because I am wood. O, Argustal, you know not the pains of wood!'

Argustal did not indeed, for long before this gnarled speech was spent, the moon had risen and the silent muddy night had fallen, and he was curled asleep in David's distorted branches, the stone in his deep pockets.

Twice more he slept, twice more watched their painful progress along unswept tracks, twice more joined converse with the melancholy tree—and when he woke again, all the heavens were stacked with fleecy cloud that showed blue between, and low hills lay ahead. He jumped down. Grass grew here. Pebbles littered the track. He howled and shouted with pleasure.

Crying his thanks he set off across the heath.

'. . . growth . . .' said David-by-the-moat-that-dries.

The heath collapsed and gave way to sand, fringed by sharp grass that scythed at Argustal's skirts as he went by. He ploughed across the sand. This was his own country, and he rejoiced, taking bearing from the occasional cairn that pointed a finger of shade across the sand. Once, one of the Forces flew over, so that for a moment of terror the world was plunged in night, thunder growled, and a paltry hundred drops of rain spattered down, then it was already on the far confines of the sun's domain, plunging away—no matter where!

Few animals, fewer birds, still survived. In the sweet deserts of Outer Talembil they were especially rare. Yet Argustal passed a bird sitting on a cairn, its hooded eye bleared with a million years of danger. It fluttered one wing at sight of him, in tribute to old reflexes, but he respected the hunger in his belly too much to try to dine on sinews and feathers, and the bird appeared to recognize the fact.

He was nearing home. The memory of Pamitar was sharp before him, so that he could follow it like a scent. He passed another of his kind, an old ape wearing a red mask hanging almost to the ground; they barely gave each other a nod of recognition. Soon on the idle skyline he saw blocks that marked Gornilo, the first town of Talembil.

The ulcerated sun travelled across the sky. Stoically, Argustal travelled across the intervening dunes, and arrived in the shadow of the white blocks of Gornilo.

No one could recollect now—recollection was one of the lost things that many felt privileged to lose—what factors had determined certain features of Gornilo's architecture. This was an ape-human town, and perhaps in order to construct a memorial to yet more distant and dreadful things, the first inhabitants of the town had made slaves of themselves and of the other creatures that now showed signs of weathering, as if they tired at last of swinging their shadows every day about their bases. The ape-humans who lived here were the same ape-humans who had lived here; they sat as untiringly under their mighty memorial blocks as they had always done—calling now to Argustal as he passed as languidly as one flicks stones across the surface of a lake—but they could recollect no longer if or how they had shifted the blocks across the desert; it might be that forgetfulness formed an integral part of being as permanent as the granite of the blocks.

Beyond the blocks stood the town. Some of the trees here were visitors, bent on becoming as David-by-the-moat-that-dries was, but most grew in the old way, content with ground and indifferent to motion. They knotted their branches this way and slatted their twigs that way, and humped their trunks the other way, and thus schemed up ingenious and ever-changing homes for the tree-going inhabitants of Gornilo.

At last Argustal came to his home, on the far side of the town.

The name of his home was Cormok. He pawed and patted and licked it first before running lightly up its trunk to the living-room.

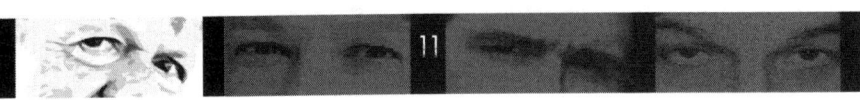

Pamitar was not there.

He was not surprised at this, hardly even disappointed, so serene was his mood. He walked slowly about the room, sometimes swinging up to the ceiling in order to view it better, licking and sniffing as he went, chasing the after-images of his wife's presence. Finally, he laughed and fell into the middle of the floor.

'Settle down, boy!' he said.

Sitting where he had dropped, he unloaded his pockets taking out the five stones he had acquired in his travels, and laying them aside from his other possessions. Still sitting, he disrobed, enjoying doing it inefficiently. Then he climbed into the sand bath.

While Argustal lay there, a great howling wind sprang up, and in a moment the room was plunged into sickly greyness. A prayer went up outside, a prayer flung by the people at the unheeding Forces not to destroy the sun. His lower lip moved in a gesture at once of content and contempt; he had forgotten the prayers of Talembil. This was a religious city. Many of the animals whose minds had dragged them aslant from what they were into rococo forms that more exactly defined their inherent qualities, until they resembled forgotten or extinct forms, or forms that had no being till now, and acknowledged no common cause with any other living thing—except in this desire to preserve the festering sunlight from further ruin.

Under the fragrant grains of the bath, submerged all but for head and a knee and hand, Argustal opened wide his perceptions to all that might come: and finally thought only what he had often thought while lying there—for the armouries of cerebration had long since been emptied of all new ammunition, whatever the tree-men of Or might claim—that in such baths, under such an unpredictable wind, the major life forms of Earth, men and trees, had probably first come at their impetus to change. But change itself... had there been a much older thing blowing about the world that everyone had forgotten?

For some reason, that question aroused discomfort in him. He felt dimly that there was another side of life than content and happiness; all beings felt content and happiness; but were those qualities a unity, or were they not perhaps one side only of a—of a shield?

He growled. Start thinking gibberish like that and you ended up human with antlers on your shoulders!

Brushing off the sand, he climbed from the bath, moving more swiftly than he had done in countless time, sliding out of his home, down to the ground without bothering to put on his clothes.

He knew where to find Pamitar. She would be beyond the town, guarding the parapatterner from the tattered angry beggars of Talembil.

The cold wind blew, with an occasional slushy thing in it that made a being blink and wonder about going on. As he strode through the green and swishing heart of Gornilo, treading among the howlers who knelt casually everywhere in rude prayer, Argustal looked up at the sun. It was visible by fragments, torn through tree and cloud. Its face was blotched and pimpled, sometimes obscured altogether for an instant at a time, then blazing forth again. It sparked like a blazing blind eye. A wind seemed to blow from it that blistered the skin and chilled the blood.

So Argustal came to his own patch of land, clear of the green town, out in the stirring desert, and to his wife, Pamitar, to the rest of the world called Miram. She squatted with her back to the wind, the sharply flying grains of sand cutting about her hairy ankles. A few paces away, one of the beggars pranced among Argustal's stones.

Pamitar stood up slowly, removing the head shawl from her head.

'Tapmar!' she said.

Into his arms he wrapped her, burying his face in her shoulder. They chirped and clucked at each other, so engrossed that they made no note of when the breeze died and the desert lost its motion and the sun's light improved.

When she felt him tense, she held him more loosely. At a hidden signal, he jumped away from her, jumping almost over her shoulder, springing ragingly forth, bowling over the lurking beggar into the sand.

The creature sprawled, two-sided and misshapen, extra arms growing from arms, head like a wolf, back legs bowed like a gorilla, clothed in a hundred textures, yet not unlovely. It laughed as it rolled and called in a high clucking voice, 'Three men sprawling under a lilac tree and none to hear the first one say, 'Ere the crops crawl, blows fall', and the second abed at night with mooncalves, answer me what's the name of the third, feller?'

'Be off with you, you mad old crow!'

And as the old crow ran away, it called out its answer, laughing, 'Why Tapmar, for he talks to nowhere!', confusing the words as it tumbled over the dunes and made its escape.

Argustal and Pamitar turned back to each other, vying with the strong sunlight to search out each other's faces, for both had forgotten when they were last together, so long was time, so dim was memory. But there were memories, and as he searched they came back. The flatness of her nose, the softness of her nostrils, the roundness of her eyes and their brownness, the curve of the rim of her lips: all these, because they were dear, became remembered, thus taking on more than beauty.

They talked gently to each other, all the while looking. And slowly something of that other thing he suspected on the dark side of the shield entered him—for her beloved countenance was not as it had been. Round her eyes, particularly under them, were shadows, and faint lines creased from the sides of her mouth. In her stance too, did not the lines flow more downward than heretofore?

The discomfort growing too great, he was forced to speak to Pamitar of these things, but there was no proper way to express them, and she seemed not to understand, unless she understood and did not know it, for her manner grew agitated, so that he soon forwent questioning, and turned to the parapatterner to hide his unease.

It stretched over mile of sand, and rose several feet into the air. From each of his long expeditions, he brought back no more than five stones, yet there were assembled here many hundreds of thousands of stones, perhaps millions, all painstakingly arranged, so that no being could take in the arrangement from any one position, not even Argustal. Many were supported in the air at various heights by stakes or poles, more lay on the ground, where Pamitar always kept the dust and the wild men from encroaching them, and of these on the ground, some stood isolated, while others lay in profusion, but all in a pattern that was ever apparent only to Argustal—and he feared that it would take him until the next sunset to have that pattern clear in his head again. Yet already it started to come clearer, and he recalled with wonder the devious and fugal course he had taken, walking down to the ravine of the tree-men of Or, and knew that he still contained the skill to place the new stones he had brought within the general pattern with reference to that natural harmony—completing the parapatterner.

And the lines on his wife's face: would they too have a place within the pattern?

Was there sense in what the crow beggar had cried, that he talked to nowhere? And... and... the terrible and, would nowhere answer him?

Bowed, he took his wife's arm and scurried back with her to their home, high in the leafless tree.

'My Tapmar,' she said that evening, as they ate a dish of fruit, 'it is good that you come back to Gornilo, for the town sedges up with dreams like an old river bed, and I am afraid.'

At this he was secretly alarmed, for the figure of speech she used seemed to him an apt one for the newly-observed lines on her face, so that he asked her what the dreams were in a voice more timid than he meant to use.

Looking at him strangely, she said, 'The dreams are as thick as fur, so thick that they congeal my throat to tell you of them. Last night, I dreamed I walked in a landscape that seemed to be clad in fur all round the distant horizons, fur that branched and sprouted and had sombre tones of russet and dun and black and a lustrous black-blue. I tried to resolve this strange material into the more familiar shapes of hedges and old distorted trees, but it stayed as it was, and I became... well, I had the word in my dream that I became a *child*.'

Argustal looked aslant over the crowded vegetation of the town and said, 'These dreams may not be of Gornilo but you only, Pamitar. What is *child*?'

'There's no such thing in reality, to my knowledge, but in the dream the child that was I was small and fresh and in its actions at once nimble and clumsy. It was alien from me, its motions and ideas never mine—and yet it was all familiar to me, I was it, Tapmar, I was that child. And now that I wake, I become sure that I once was such a thing as a *child*.'

He tapped his fingers on his knees, shaking his head and blinking in a sudden anger. 'This is your bad secret, Pamitar! I knew you had one the moment I saw you! I read it in your face which has changed in an evil way! You know you were never anything but Pamitar in all the million of years of your life, and that *child* must be an evil phantom that possesses you. Perhaps you will now be turned into a *child*!'

She cried out and hurled green fruit into which she had bitten. Deftly, he caught it before it struck him.

They made provisional peace before settling for sleep. That night, Argustal dreamed that he also was small and vulnerable and hardly able to manage the language; his intentions were like an arrow and his direction clear.

Waking, he sweated and trembled, for he knew that as he had been *child* in his dream, so he had been *child* once in life. And this went deeper than sickness. When his pained looks directed themselves outside, he saw the night was like shot silk, with a dappled effect of light and shadow in the dark blue dome of the sky, which signified that the Forces were making merry with the sun while it journeyed through the Earth; and Argustal thought of his journeys across the Earth, and of his visit to Or, when the tree-men had whispered of an unknown element that forces change.

'They prepared me for this dream!' he muttered. He knew now that change had worked in his very foundations; once, he had been this thin tiny alien thing called *child*, and his wife too, and possibly others. He thought of that little apparition again, with its spindly legs and piping voice; the horror of it chilled his heart; he broke into prolonged groans that all Pamitar's comforting took a long part of the dark to silence.

He left her sad and pale. He carried with him the stones he had gathered on his journey, the odd-shaped one from the ravine at Or and the ones he had acquired before that. Holding them tightly to him, Argustal made his way through the town to his spatial arrangement. For so long, it had been his chief preoccupation; today, the long project would come to completion; yet because he could not even say why it had so preoccupied him, his feelings inside lay flat and wretched. Something had got to him and killed content.

Inside the prospects of the parapatterner, the old beggarly man lay, resting his shaggy head on a blue stone. Argustal was too low in spirit to chase him away.

'As your frame of stones will frame words, the words will come forth stones,' cried the creature.

'I'll break your bones, old crow!' growled Argustal, but inwardly he wondered at this vile crow's saying and at what he had said the previous day about Argustal's talking to nowhere, for Argustal had discussed the purpose of his structure with nobody, not even Pamitar. Indeed, he had not recognized the purpose

The Worm That Flies

of the structure himself until two journeys back—or had it been three or four? The pattern had started simply as a pattern (hadn't it?) and only much later had the obsession become on purpose.

To place the new stones correctly took time. Wherever Argustal walked in his great framework, the old crow followed, sometimes on two legs, sometimes on four. Other personages from the town collected to stare, but none dared step inside the perimeter of the structure, so that they remained far off, like little stalks growing on the margins of Argustal's mind.

Some stones had to touch, others had to be just apart. He walked and stooped and walked, responding to the great pattern that he now knew contained a universal law. The task wrapped him round in an aesthetic daze similar to the one he had experienced travelling the labyrinthine way down to Or, but with greater intensity.

The spell was broken only when the old crow spoke from a few paces away in a voice level and unlike his usual sing-song. And the old crow said, 'I remember you planting the very first of these stones here when you were a child.'

Argustal straightened.

Cold took him, though the bilious sun shone bright. He could not find his voice. As he searched for it, his gaze went across to the eyes of the beggar-man, festering in his black forehead.

'You know I was once such a phantom—a child?' he asked.

'We are all phantoms. We were all childs. As there is gravy in our bodies, our hours were once few.'

'Old crow... you describe a different world—not ours!'

'Very true, very true. Yet that other world once was ours.'

'Oh, not! Not so!'

'Speak to your machine about it! Its tongue is of rock and cannot lie like mine.' He picked up a stone and flung it. 'That will I do! Now get away from me!'

The stone hit the old man in his ribs. He groaned painfully and danced backwards, tripped, was up again, and made off in haste, limbs whirling in a way that took from him all resemblance to human kind. He pushed through the line of watchers and was gone.

For a while, Argustal squatted where he was, groping through matters that dissolved as they took shape, only to grow large when he dismissed them. The storm blew through him and distorted him, like the trouble on the face of the sun. When he decided there was nothing for it but to complete the para-patterner, still he trembled with the new knowledge: without being able to understand why, he knew that the new knowledge would destroy the old world.

All now was in position, save for the odd-shaped stone from Or, which he carried firm on one shoulder, tucked between ear and hand. For the first time, he realized what a gigantic structure he had wrought. It was a business-like stroke of insight, no sentiment involved. Argustal was now no more than a bead rolling through the vast interstices around him.

Each stone held its own temporal record as well as its special position; each represented different stresses, different epochs, different temperatures, materials, chemicals, moulds, intensities. Every stone together represented an anagram of Earth, its whole composition and continuity. The last stone was merely a focal point for an entire dynamic and, as Argustal slowly walked between the vibrant arcades, that dynamic rose to pitch.

He heard it grow. He paused. He shuffled now this way, now that. As he did so, he recognized that there was no one focal position but a myriad, depending on position and direction of the key stone.

Very softly, he said '... That my fears might be verified...'

And all about him—but softly—came a voice in stone, stuttering before it grew clearer, as if it had long known of words but never practised them.

'Thou...' Silence, then a flood of sentence.

'Thou thou art, O thou art worm thou art sick, rose invisible rose. In the howling storm though art in the storm. Worm thou art found out O rose thou art sick and found out flies in the night they bed they thy crimson life destroy. O—O rose, thou art sick! The invisible worm, the invisible worm that flies in the night, in the howling storm, has found out—had found out thy bed of crimson joy... and his dark dark secret love, his dark secret love does thy life destroy.'

Argustal was already running from that place.

In Pamitar's arms he could find no comfort now. Though he huddled there, up in the encaging branches, the worm that flies worked in him. Finally, he rolled away from her and said, 'Who ever heard so terrible voice? I cannot speak again with the universe.'

'You do not know it was the universe.' She tried to tease him. 'Why should the universe speak to little Tapmar?'

'The old crow said I spoke to nowhere. Nowhere is the universe—where the sun hides at night—where our memories hide, where our thoughts evaporate. I cannot talk with it. I must hunt out the old crow and talk to him.'

'Talk no more, ask no more question! All you discover brings you misery! Look—you will no longer regard me, your poor wife! You turn your eyes away!'

'If I stare at nothing for all succeeding eons, yet I must find out what torments us!'

In the centre of Gornilo, where many of the Unclassified lived, bare wood twisted up from the ground like fossilized sack, creating caves and shelters and strange limbs on which and in which old pilgrims, otherwise without a home, might perch. Here at nightfall Argustal sought out the beggar.

The old fellow was stretched painfully beside a broken pot, clasping a woven garment across his body. He turned in his small cell, trying for escape, but Argustal had him by the throat and held him still.

'I want your knowledge, old crow!'

'Get it from the religious men—they know more than I!'

It made Argustal pause, but he slackened his grip on the other by only the smallest margin.

'Because I have you, you must speak to me. I know that knowledge is pain, but so is ignorance once one has sensed its presence. Tell me more about childs and what they did!'

As if in a fever, the old crow rolled about under Argustal's grip. He brought himself to say, 'What I know is so little, so little, like a blade of grass in a field. And like blades of grass are the distant bygone times. Through all those times come the bundles of bodies now on this Earth. Then as now, no new bodies. But once... even before those bygone times... you cannot understand...'

'I understand well enough.'

'You are Scientist! Before bygone times was another time, and then... then was childs and different things that are not any longer, many animals and birds and smaller things with frail wings unable to carry them over long time...'

'What happened? Why was there change, old crow?'

'Men... scientists... make understanding of the gravy of bodies and turn every person and thing and tree to eternal life. We now continue from that time, a long time long—so long we forgotten what was then done.'

The smell of him was like an old pie. Argustal asked him, 'And why now are no childs?'

'Childs are just small adults. We are adults, having become from child. But in that great former time, before scientists were on Earth, adults produced childs. Animals and trees likewise. But with eternal life, this cannot be—those child-making parts of the body have less life than stone.'

'Don't talk of stone! So we live forever... You old ragbag, you remember—ah, you remember me as child?'

But the old ragbag was working himself into a kind of fit, pummelling the ground, slobbering at the mouth.

'Seven shades of lilac, even worse I remember myself a child, running like an arrow, air, everywhere fresh rosy air. So I am mad, for I remember!' He began to scream and cry, and the outcast round about took up the wail in chorus. 'We remember, we remember!'—whether they did or not.

Their dreadful howling worked like spears in Argustal's flank. He had pictures afterwards of his panic run through the town, of wall and trunk and ditch and road, but it was all as insubstantial at the time as the pictures afterwards. When he finally fell to the ground panting, he was unaware of where he lay, and everything was nothing to him until the religious howling had died into silence.

Then he saw he lay in the middle of his great structure, his cheek against the Or stone where he had dropped it. And as his attention came to it, the great structure round him answered without his having to speak.

He was at a new focal point. The voice that sounded was new, as cool as the previous one had been choked. It blew over him in a cool wind.

'There is no amaranth on this side of the grave, O Argustal, no name with whatsoever emphasis of passionate love repeated that is not mute at last. Experiment X gave life for eternity to every living thing on Earth, but even eternity is punctuated by release and suffers period. The old life had its childhood and its end, the new had no such logic. It found its own after many millennia, and took its cue from individual minds. What a man was, he became; what a tree, it became.'

Argustal lifted his tired head from its pillow of stone. Again the voice changed pitch and trend, as if in response to his minute gesture.

'The present is a not in music. That note can no longer be sustained. You find what questions you have found, O Argustal, because the chord, in dropping to a lower key, rouses you from the long dream of crimson joy that was immortality. What you are finding, others also find, and you can none of you be any longer insensible to change. Even immortality must have an end.'

He stood up then, and hurled the Or stone. It flew, fell, rolled ... and before it stopped he had awoken a great chorus of universal voice.

The whole Earth roused, and a wind blew from the west. As he started again to move, he saw the religious men of the town were on the march, and the great sun-nesting Forces on their midnight wing, and the stars wheeling, and every majestic object alert as it had never been.

But Argustal walked slowly on his flat simian feet, plodding back to Pamitar. No longer would he be impatient in her arms. There, time would be all too brief.

He knew now the worm that flew and nestled in her cheek, in his cheek, in all things, even in the tree-men of Or, even in the great impersonal Forces that despoiled the sun, even in the sacred bowels of the universe to which he had lent a temporary tongue. He knew now that back had come that Majesty that previously gave to Life its reason, the Majesty that had been away from the world for so long and yet so brief respite, the Majesty called DEATH.

Joanne Harris

Waiting for Gandalf

JOANNE HARRIS

Because sometimes, reality just doesn't satisfy.

It's not always fun being a monster. I mean, someone has to do it, and sometimes you can have a bit of a laugh beating up an elf or a wizard, but let's face it, most of the time it's all about lurking behind bushes or knee deep in icy water, waiting for the adventurers to stumble upon you by accident, or, more likely, to pass you by altogether and move on to the next encounter, leaving you to freeze your butt off till someone remembers to tell you where they've gone.

Of course, they don't tell you that at first. Monstering's the best job, that's what they say. No guilt, no stress, cool gear and the ability to come back to life on demand. What else could you need?

Well, maybe it *does* have its moments. I remember my first time: sixteen years old; bookish; skinny; desperate.

There was a girl in it: a half-elf; twenty years old; red hair and little latex ears. Gorgeous. In fact I'd joined the group just to be near her, though she hardly ever noticed me except occasionally to shoot arrows at me or to hack at me with her sword. Still, she always killed me in an affectionate, friendly way, or so I told myself, and in return I always made a special effort when I was attacking her, until she complained that she was being harassed and her boyfriend (a pro warrior with quarterback shoulders and a bad case of testosterone) had to warn me off.

Four for Fantasy

By then, though, I was hooked. I'd been bashed, battered, hacked, decapitated, blessed, shot, levitated, zombified, vaporized, stabbed, turned and reduced to slime. And still every Saturday night I came back, come rain, come snow, to spend the midnight hours in combat against the forces of light.

Such is the demonic lure of the live-action role playing game. You start with Tolkien—maybe your school even encourages you—then, slowly drawn in via Steve Jackson or Games Workshop, your habit becomes secretive: sinister. Your parents complain that you never go out, of strange smells coming from your room. Your friends avoid you; you find yourself hanging around Oxfam shops; you begin to appreciate what your little sister sees in *Xena, Warrior Princess*; and finally you erupt triumphantly onto the scene clad in a woolly jumper (sprayed silver to approximate chain mail) and with your bedroom curtain pinned proudly around your shoulders, bearing a rubber sword coated in silver masking tape and calling yourself Scrud theMagnificent.

Predictably, this outing is greeted with fear and loathing by your loved ones. But already the seed is sown; you enter the world of hardcore role-play, and within three weeks you've exchanged your taped sword for one moulded from latex, you're making your own chain mail from thousands of split washers and you find yourself debating the relative merits of cap or raglan sleeves with a dwarf called Snorri.

From then on, there's no turning back. Every Saturday night, the role-playing cell—a party of adventurers, one of monsters and a monster referee—convenes at the edge of the woods. Throughout the night these warring factions pursue one another through the undergrowth, armed to the fangs and bent on murder. It's an addiction, you see; the dark, the thrill of the hunt, the primitive weapons, the primal fear. And for some—for the weaklings like myself, for the desperate, for the rejects and the misfits and the loners and the freaks—it provides much-needed relief; a chance, for a night, to be something other than themselves.

Two weeks out of three I was a monster. The third week I was a warrior priest by the name of Lazar, until I was shot by a group of orcs; then I was a ranger called Wayland, who managed to reach third level before falling into an ambush set by an evil cleric; then a wizard called Doomcaster, unexpectedly hit by a magic missile; and finally a barbarian called Snod who had to be abandoned on grounds of ill-health (it was January, kneedeep in snow, and barbarians don't wear vests).

For some time I put it down to bad luck that my characters so seldom survived the night. Other regulars advanced, gained levels and skills, became in fact almost invulnerable. Thirty years later, most of the regulars are still with us: there's Titania, the elf-maid, still red-haired and gorgeous; Litso the thief; Beltane the warrior, who tells everyone he's in the Territorial Army at weekends; Philbert Silvermane the old paladin, over forty when we started and still going strong—though he tends to go for less combat nowadays, and more elixir from his potion flask. Snorri the axe-man is still with us, and Jupitus the wizard, and Veldarron the swordsman, and Morag the healer, who only comes along because she's Veldarron's girlfriend and he's always getting hurt. In fact he can hardly pick up a sword without hitting himself in the face with it, but thanks to Morag's healing skills, he's managed to achieve both virtual immortality and a long-standing reputation as a master of weaponry.

I'm not sure about Morag's commitment, though. Frankly, it's rather dull being a healer. I've seen her face when she thinks the others aren't looking, and she has this habit of saying 'Yeah, whatever' when someone corrects her incantations. Still, Veldarron's always had a bit of a thing for Titania (doesn't everyone?), and I suppose Morag thinks she's keeping an eye on the competition. And finally, there's Spider. I have to say I'm a little worried about him; I mean, there's fantasy, and there's real life, but I'm not sure Spider knows the difference. For a start, I've never seen him out of character. The others have daytime identities: Titania runs a New Age bookshop; Veldarron's an accountant; Litso works for the Inland Revenue. But not Spider. As far as anyone can tell, he's Spider all the time. No one knows his real name; no one has ever seen him out of costume. The others come along in combats or jeans, exchange pleasantries, maybe drop in at a nearby pub for a couple of beers before they get kitted up and into the part. But not Spider. He doesn't do small talk. Ask him if he watched the film on TV last night and he'll just give you one of his long stares, as if you're something he's just found under a stone. No one knows where he lives. You can't imagine him living in a regular house, with a sofa or a toaster or even a bed. He'll meet you in the pub—he'll even have a drink if someone else is paying—but he'll always arrive in full kit: swords, crossbow, cloak, ring mail, backpack, tunic, potions flask, utility

belt, holy symbol. And it's good gear—professional gear. Everyone else has mostly homemade stuff. Most of the players have one good and fairly authentic item—usually a weapon. But *all* Spider's stuff looks authentic.

Ring mail, for instance, costs a fortune; but fitted, customized ring mail costs more. You can pay up to three hundred pounds for a really good latex weapon, but Spider has a whole armoury of them: long swords, bastard swords, short swords, shields, daggers, crossbows with special bolts; plus the real weapons he carries just for show (obviously he can't use them in combat). Great for role-play, but it does tend to cause a bit of a stir down the local on a Saturday night.

Not that he cares. He's immune to mockery or funny looks. And since that incident with the football crowd last summer, most people give him a wide berth, and avoid those tempting *Lord of the Rings* jokes. Because unlike Veldarron, Spider *can* fight; as a perpetual monster, I can vouch for that. He practises, you see. In thirty years, I've seen him injured less than a dozen times. And when it does happen he takes it so *seriously*, with vials of fake blood and stage-make-up scars. What's more, I suspect he has them tattooed on afterwards—I know for a fact that he still has the scar I gave him five years ago, from a magic missile, when I was an evil cleric. Latex sword or not, he looked ready to kill me for hitting him in the back, but Titania—whose turn it was to be the ref that night—decided it was a fair shot and First Morag (one of our present Morag's predecessors) had to heal him quick. Since then I've been a little bit nervous of Spider.

Then, of course, we've got the monsters. Tonight there are ten of us; mostly occasional players, not regulars like Titania, Spider and me. The university's a good place to look for sword-fodder; most students have plenty of time on their hands, and they're cheerful, energetic and, for the most part, easy to manage. Still, it's important to have an experienced person in charge; that's why I'm here. New monsters can sometimes get carried away: they don't declare hits; they get over-excited. I'm here to keep them under control. To make sure they follow the rules. To make sure no one *really* gets killed. Because in those woods anything can happen; it's dark, you're edgy, and sometimes on a good night you can genuinely believe it's all for real; that there really are orcs out there, or werewolves, or walking dead. Out there you can almost believe you're miles from civilization; your only light is the moon; every shadow might be an enemy. One false move, and you're dead; the knowledge leaves every nerve-end sizzling, every sense aware.

On a bad night, it's raining; you've sprained your ankle; there's dogshit on your adventuring boots and you can hear faint karaoke from a nearby pub; then a police car draws up to investigate a report of a disturbance and as the most experienced member of the group, you're left trying to explain to the duty constable precisely *why* you're traipsing round the woods at one in the morning dressed as a goblin and covered in mud. Like I said, it's not always fun being a monster.

Tonight's a little mixed. OK, it's raining a little. But there are raggy clouds overhead, and a quarter moon, and it's not too cold. Atmospheric. Right now I'm sitting under a tree with my cagoule on, going over the encounter sheets. It's my turn to monster ref. I'm quite looking forward to that.

The monsters are here already. You have to brief them first, when the regular players aren't around, so that they know more or less what's going to happen and what costumes they have to wear. There are roles to allocate, rules to lay down. Often there's a newbie, some spotty student in Army gear who fancies his chances. Tonight there are three, all a bit giggly and hyperactive. I don't know their names—sometimes there's no point in learning them, as turnover can be quite rapid. The others are sixth-form pupils of mine, aged seventeen or eighteen at the most: Matt, Pete, Stuart, Scott, Jase and Andy. And me, of course. Smithy. The perpetual monster.

Well, of course I'm aware that to them I'm a bit of a joke. Forty-six; skinny; balding; desperate. I'm aware that out of costume I look exactly like a geography teacher—which is just as well, because that's what I am—and I've noticed the embarrassed silence that sometimes falls when I come over to the group, and seen the looks exchanged by the newbies when they think I can't see them. Poor old Smithy, that's what they're thinking; always three steps behind. God help me, what a loser. God help me if I ever get that sad.

But there's a kind of glory in the old moves. *They* won't understand that, being eighteen and immortal; but I do. They think it's only a game; in a couple of weeks they'll have found another game to play, or worse still, formed a splinter group with kids their own age, bending the rules and having a laugh. I try to tell them, this isn't *about* having a laugh. They think we do it for the gear; that we're just a group of fetishists and Luddites, like people who go around in Star Trek uniforms, or live in tepees with sheep and no central heating.

But it isn't about gear, either. It's about honour, and rules, and good and evil. It's about death and glory. And it's about the *truth*—not the truth that dragons exist, but the fact that they can be defeated. Because, more than ever with the passing of time, I want to believe that they *can* be defeated. Philbert knows what I mean—his wife died of cancer twenty years ago, and we're all he has left. So does Titania, childless and pushing fifty; and Litso, who spends his whole life—bar these Saturday nights—pretending to be straight. Those kids have no idea; no idea what it's like to come home to my other, sad, imaginary life—two rooms, a three-bar fire and a sleeping cat; to be known as Sad Smithy by generations of geography students; to lie awake at night with a knot in my stomach, looking out at the electric stars—every one a window, every one a home. But it's what Spider says—when he says anything, which isn't that often. Those things are not for us, he says. House, wife, kids. Those things are for the Mundanes. Regular people. People with imaginary lives.

'How much longer?' That was one of the newbies, looking at his watch. You must know the type: impatient, nervy, scornful, cold; only here because someone (myself, perhaps) hinted at something dangerous—something occult and forbidden.

'Not long now.' Come to think of it, they *are* a little late; it's eleven o'clock and dead quiet. 'Get your gear.'

He shoots me a contemptuous look and pulls on his mask. It's latex and pretty realistic—I make them myself, and they're much better than the bought ones. I find myself hoping he gets killed first.

"Cause I could have got lucky tonight,' says the newbie in a muffled voice. 'There's a bird down the Woolpack keeps givin' me the eye.'

It's sad, really. We both know his life. We both know he'll never get lucky. But there's no time to discuss it; I can see a shadow coming out of the trees, and from the noise he's making—and the size of the sword slung across his back—it has to be Veldarron. Morag's with him, looking tired and displeased—they've probably been fighting again. Still, I'm glad they arrived first; a few of the others can sometimes come across a bit strange to newbies, and I don't want any trouble tonight. Besides, I know these students; half of them are only here because they think they're going to get off with some leather-clad warrior babe, and although Morag isn't exactly Xena material, at least she *is* female—and at twenty-nine, rather closer to their generation than the rest of us.

I greet them with the usual mantra—'Today is a good day to die,'—in the hope of getting them both into the fighting mood. But as the couple come closer, I can see that all is not well with Morag. Her face is set, her lips tight, and worse still, she has come out of character, in jeans and a parka rather than her customary robes and healer's hood. Damn it, I think. And damn Veldarron, who is making a point of not being with her, making showy practice moves to a dead tree and waiting for me to sort things out, as usual.

'What's wrong?' I ask Morag. 'Why aren't you kitted up?'

'I'm not staying, Smithy.'

'Why not?'

Morag just looks at me, and I feel my heart sink. Of course it isn't the first time that one of Veldarron's girlfriends has pulled out at a crucial moment (he's an insensitive bastard, and I really don't understand what girls see in him), but to lose a healer, our only healer, and at eleven o'clock on a Saturday night, presents a crisis of major proportions. 'But we need you,' I manage at last. 'I've got an adventure to run, and they'll be wanting a healer.'

'Can't help that,' says Morag, shrugging. 'I quit. Tell Darren to get himself another patsy. This one's out of here.'

'But Morag—'

She turns on me then, unexpectedly. 'My name's *not* bloody Morag!' she yells. 'Six years I've been coming here, Smithy, and you don't even know my sodding *name!*'

Well, talk about volatile. Why on earth should I know her name, I ask myself, as I watch her stalk away across the moonlit clearing. What's more, after six years she should know that you never—*never*—refer to an adventurer by his real name during a session. No wonder Veldarron looks so put out. Still—though I'm sure he'll manage to recruit another Morag before next week—her unexpected departure suddenly makes everything much more difficult for me, as I have quite a challenging bunch of young monsters lined up for tonight's adventure. In any case, it's far too late to change anything now; all we can hope for is a short session, good luck, orderly monsters and no more unpleasant surprises.

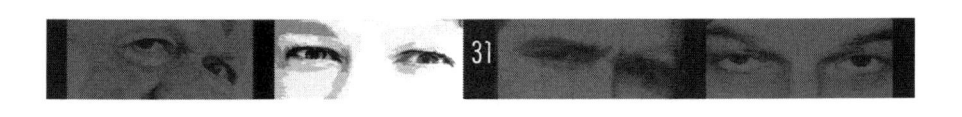

I can see the rest of the party arriving now, with Philbert in the lead. Philbert Silvermane, he calls himself, though we all know that hair's a wig. Tonight I think he looks smaller than usual, bent beneath the weight of his armour, although in the moonlight he still looks rather fine. There's a certain nobility in that proud old head, like a ruined arch standing in the middle of a field, purposeless, but not without grace. Of course I didn't always think so; I was young once, and I'm ashamed to say I often sniggered—in the days when forty seemed impossibly old.

Sure enough, I think I hear laughter from one of the newbies. Philbert doesn't hear—he's a little deaf—but I'm already on edge after the business with Morag, and it makes me feel irrationally angry. I snap out a sharp command to the monsters, lining them up behind the big bush as the adventurers begin to assemble. There's Litso, in drag as usual; Beltane in very un-medieval combats under his tabard; Jupitus, slow and heavy in his long wizard's robes; Snorri with his axe.

More laughter from the newbies. I expected it; some of those outfits probably look quite comic to them, especially Litso, with his laddered fishnets and leather skirt. But tonight it galls me. Perhaps because of Morag; perhaps because I'm in charge; perhaps because it is not entirely kind. The newbies are in for a hard time, anyway. I don't like their attitude. Neither does Litso. We have a rule here that no one comments on another player's persona, however bizarre—Philbert (who was a psychology professor in another life) says it's because the role-play is cathartic, allowing the individual to act out fantasies which, if repressed, might be damaging to the ego. During these sessions we banish guilt, fear and mockery, emerging cleansed and renewed. I almost say as much to the newbies, but there isn't time; that's Spider stepping dead-silent out of the undergrowth, and in his wake, finally, Titania.

Titania. As always, my heart does a little skip. Because she hasn't changed; not really. Her costume has had to be altered a few times to account for her expanding waistline, but to me she's still lovely, her red hair loose over her shoulders, her light sword in her hand.

Someone says something behind me. I can't quite hear what it is, but it sounds derogatory. I look round rapidly, but I see only blank faces. Our regular monsters—Matt, Pete, Stuart, Scott, Jase and Andy—wear expressions of studious unconcern; the newbie who complained of waiting is drumming his fingers, but apart from that everyone is still. Good. At least they have the sense not to laugh in front of Spider.

It's raining now. Spider doesn't mind; as he steps into the little clearing by the side of the big bush I can see the droplets collecting in his braided hair. I hand him the briefing sheet—it's written in runes, as Spider won't read ordinary script—and lead the monster party beyond the clearing to set up the first encounter.

The voices of the adventurers reach me across the clearing. They are discussing the loss of their healer, reworking their strategy, re-allocating salves and potions.

'Right, listen,' I tell the monsters. 'Tonight you'll all have to take especial care. We're a player down and we don't have anyone to stand in, so it's all the more important that we do our job properly and don't get carried away. For this first encounter, you're all ghouls, three hits each, so put your masks on and get into position.' I take time to look closely at all the monsters, especially the newbies, who are standing by looking keyed up and fidgety. 'Remember,' I tell them, 'it's three hits each. No more. There's no healer in this party, and I don't want any fatalities on this adventure.'

Someone gives a snort of laughter—one of the newbies, the restless one who complained of waiting.

'What is it?' I make my voice sharp.

'Nothing.' He manages to make even a single word sound insulting.

I'd like to teach him a lesson. But there isn't time; besides, he'll be laughing on the other side of his face in a minute. The thought makes me feel a little better. The ghouls are concealed in the bushes, but not well; ghouls are relatively slow-moving, stupid creatures who should present little challenge. A warm-up battle, that's all; something to get the juices flowing. I blow the whistle. Time in.

This is the moment—the secret, exhilarating rush. It's the reason we play; the reason we've always played. Far more than just a game, it goes beyond catharsis. These youngsters do not feel it as we do, Titania, Philbert, Spider and I. It is intoxicating. It is magical. To be heroes, like in the David Bowie song; to be beyond age, beyond time; to be (for a minute, an hour, a night) one of the immortals.

Ah. Here comes the party. Beltane and Veldarron heading the group, Spider covering the rear, Litso scouting ahead. The monsters are ready, the restless newbie creeping quietly around the back of the party with rather more skill than a ghoul normally shows. Still, he's making an effort; I can hardly penalize him for that.

One of our regulars strikes first. It's Pete, playing his part conscientiously with arms outstretched and shambling walk. Scott joins him, then Andy, cutting off Litso from the rest of the party and forcing him to fight them three at a time. This is where the fighters come into their own; but Beltane is already fighting Jase and Matt, and Veldarron—conscious, perhaps, of Morag's absence—is keeping his distance.

The newbies are hanging back—rather too strategically for ghouls—but even so, the party should be able to handle the attack with ease. Litso takes a couple of hits to the right arm, always a weakness in his defence, and Veldarron gets a slash across the ribs, but for the most part the adventurers manage to repel their attackers with ease. Thirty seconds later, only the newbies are still standing. Their leader—the restless one who led the attack—is fighting quite competently against Beltane, but I find it hard to believe that he hasn't already received his three hits, and as for the others, they aren't responding to hits at all, but are simply ignoring them and trying to do as much damage as they can.

'Pull your blows!' yells Titania angrily, as she gets the flat edge of a sword smack in the face, but the three newbies do not back off. Instead, the first one yanks off his constricting mask and with a loud war cry launches himself right into the centre of the party.

'Oi! No ganging up!' shouts Veldarron, now the focus of three monsters at once. He's right, of course; it's one of the most basic game rules, and I had explained it all very clearly to the newbies, but in the heat of the moment they must have forgotten. To cap it all, Veldarron is shouting so much that his aim goes wide, and by the time Spider intervenes, cutting down the three ghouls from behind with a series of vicious thrusts, the swordsman is on the ground with several serious injuries.

The post-battle debriefing is loud and acrimonious. I have no choice but to rule Veldarron out of action, which displeases him enormously and gives rise to cheers from the monsters. Litso, too, has suffered humiliating injury, and Titania complains that she had to hit her ghoul at least twenty times before he finally agreed to lie down and die. I talk to the monsters about it, and though the regulars are polite, I don't like the newbies' attitude at all.

'Twenty hits? She must be joking. I don't think she hit me once.'

'Hits have got to be convincing. If I can't feel it, then I can't count it.'

I repeat what I have already said about counting hits and pulling blows. I'm almost sure I see the lead newbie pulling a face. 'What?' I say, for the second time.

He shrugs. 'Whatever.'

But it has soured the game. I can feel it; a tug of revolt from within the ranks. Two encounters on, the party runs into a group of bandits, which puts up far more of a fight than anticipated. Litso gets hit twice more, Philbert four times and Titania and Beltane once each, although Jupitus the wizard manages to put an end to the opposition with a crafty sequence of spells. The monsters protest a little at this, and mutter about retribution, so that once again I have to warn them about playing to the rules.

"Sonly a game,' says one of the newbies sullenly. "Snot life and death, is it?'

Oh, but it is. I wish I could make him see that, but the gulf between us is too wide. Life begins as a game, and ends in a fight to the death. I try to set up the next encounter as quickly as I can, but even so it takes time; one of the newbies begins a chorus of *Why are we waiting?*, and to my annoyance, the others join in.

By now the entire party is beginning to feel the absence of their healer. By the fifth encounter, Litso is out of action, Philbert is hardly any better, and Beltane is down to five hits. Only Spider is serene and untouched, cutting a swathe through the monsters time after time. The restless newbie looks annoyed at this, but says nothing. Spider does have that effect on people.

We have reached the seventh encounter. The party has lost no further members, although morale is low, and everyone but Spider has received some kind of injury. I feel somehow to blame, although I know it isn't my fault; some nights are better than others, that's all, and new players are always a bit of a risk. Still, I don't feel entirely in control of my little group; it makes me uneasy, as if some part of my imaginary life has managed to infiltrate this, my real one.

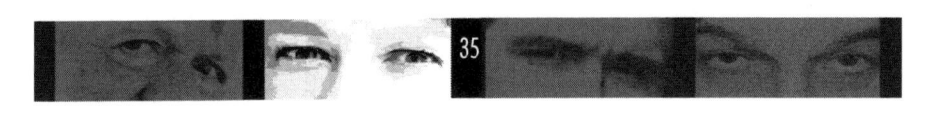

During the debriefing, one of the newbies lights a cigarette. It's against the rules, but my mood is so uncertain that I hesitate to challenge him about it. The regular monsters—Scott and Matt and Jase and the rest—seem restless too, as if some kind of signal has passed between them, and there is a great deal of murmuring and covert laughter behind my back as I go about my business. It makes me uneasy. As a teacher I know the danger a disruptive influence presents, and throughout the session I have become more and more convinced that my newbies—especially one of them – are manifestations of that unrest. They are testing me somehow, assessing my ability to react to their taunts, challenging my authority.

'Right,' I tell them crisply, handing out sheets for the next encounter. 'This time you're not hostile. You're a group of soldiers from another camp, and you'll have healing potions for the party if they can negotiate with you.'

I slipped that one in to try and solve the Morag problem. The restless newbie pulls a face, and I can see he isn't pleased at the prospect of a non-combative encounter. 'What if they attack us?' he says.

'Then you fight,' I tell him. 'But you won't instigate anything.'

'*Instigate.* What's that mean?' sneers the newbie.

I give him a look. 'You got a problem?'

He shrugs.

'I said *have you got a problem?*'

The newbie smirks in a way that manages to be both insolent and sheepish. 'Well, it's the way you all take it so seriously,' he says at last. 'Like it's real, or something. I mean, it's just a fucking *game,* for God's sake. Look at you all. There's that old git in the fright wig, and that weirdo in drag, and that fat bird—'

It is at this point that something in me breaks. Oh, people have taunted us and mocked us before; called us saddos and freaks and mutants and all that. But to hear him speak of Titania—of *my* Titania—and, even more importantly, to hear him denigrate the game—I grab hold of the first weapon that comes to hand—a longbladed bastard sword—and fall automatically into my fighting stance.

'I'll give you a game,' I tell him. 'You monster.'

The newbies look nervous and back away, but I am too angry to stop now. All I can think of is the fact that this boy—this boy!—has insulted Titania, a warrior with countless successful campaigns behind her, a woman of legendary grace and beauty, and that the insult—to her and to the rest of us—cannot go unpunished.

'Time in!' I roar. 'Party, to me!'

It is cathartic. I have never gone berserker before – some players never do, in decades of gaming, though the best ones have done it at least once, usually in the face of insuperable odds. I remember Spider once doing it, in a pub in Nottingham, in the days when people still laughed about him behind his back, and I'd tried—without success—to imagine how it must feel: the liberation, the rush, the joy. Now I know; and as my friends rush into battle to join me I know that our enemy is not this boy, this newbie with the bad manners and the foul mouth. Our enemy is something infinitely more dangerous, hateful and formidable; a creature with countless heads, all stamped with identical expressions of youthful scorn and ignorant self-absorption. For thirty years we have stalked our Adversary, without knowing quite what it was we hunted; for thirty years we have contented ourselves with second-rate alternatives, when all the time the real quarry was close enough to touch. The others sense it too; grabbing weapons left and right they join me, fighting back-to-back as in the old days—Litso flinging spears into the enemy ranks; Spider with a sword in each hand and blood running down his arm. Philbert is cut down, but we will avenge him; I catch sight of Titania's contorted face, screaming some incantation, before I plunge once more into the enemy horde.

Veldarron falls; all around me the monsters are screaming and striking—with clubs, swords, axes. I catch sight of Matt, with blood on his face, but I know him now; I know them all. They are the enemy which cannot be defeated; the sneering armies of Youth, many-headed, indestructible.

Beltane falls; Snorri is surrounded. Left and right we hew our way, unmoved by the pleas and cries of the monsters. Blows rain against my back, but I can barely feel them. Jupitus falls; then Titania, my Titania. My heart, pounding like a hammer, feels close to breaking.

Now only Spider and I are left. Our eyes meet across the battlefield, and I see an expression on his face that I have never seen before, not in thirty years of fighting together: an expression of pure and abandoned joy. For a second he holds my gaze. In that moment I feel it too; the joy, the ecstasy. Our comrades are down. The enemy is strong. But we are warriors, Spider and I. And today is a good day to die.

'No mercy!' I roar at the top of my voice, and at last I am elated to see the enemy fleeing before me—the ones who still can. Only the restless newbie stands his ground. I can see him mouthing something at me, but my ears have stopped working. His face is twisted with indecision and disbelief, and there is something at his feet, something soft that whimpers and writhes.

Spider and I take him both at once. Our swords strike in a dozen places. And it is now, as our last enemy falls and the mist drops from my eyes, that I see the blood on Spider's discarded sword, black in the moonlight, and I remember the weapons he carries for show, just for show and for the special occasions, alongside the ones so carefully built and designed for safety.

The battleground is littered with bodies; ours and theirs. Only one is not accounted for. But I knew that already. A small sound in the underbrush is the only indication of his passing; I know from experience that he will leave no trail. I find Titania lying to the side; she is dazed, but unhurt, and I help her up with a little thrill of illicit enjoyment. Beltane, too, is unhurt but for a scratch across his face; a moment or two later Litso emerges from the bushes, looking scared and relieved. Only Philbert hasn't made it, we discover later; his old heart just wasn't up to all the excitement. Still, he died in battle, as Veldarron says; and that's what matters.

'What about these monsters?' says Titania, looking down at the corpses. 'What a mess. Couldn't Spider have saved a few for next time?'

'Come on, sweetheart,' I tell her. 'It was a good fight. And we can always get a batch of fresh monsters from the Poly. In fact, there's a fantasy club just started that looks likely. Give me a week, and we'll have numbers back up to normal. Now look at me, Titania,'—I wipe a smear of blood tenderly from her cheek—'have I ever let you down? Well, have I?'

She hesitates. 'Of course you haven't, Smithy,' she said. 'It's just—' once again she looks down at the dead monsters, and her brow furrows. 'It's just that sometimes I wonder what other people—you know, *regular* people—Mundanes—would think of all this.'

I look at her in surprise. 'Mundanes? What does it matter what they think?' Reluctantly she smiles. 'Perhaps I'm getting sensitive in my old age,' she says.

'You're not old, Titania,' I tell her shyly. 'You're beautiful.'

This time her smile is more assured. She gives me a small, soft kiss on the side of the mouth. 'You're so sweet, Smithy.'

To the victor, the spoils. Her hair is slightly smoky from her time in the pub, and there is a salty taste on her lips. I kiss her, while behind me, Veldarron and the others look on with wide-open eyes and identical expressions of envy and astonishment.

'So what happens next?' That's Snorri, looking slightly troubled, his eye on the fallen monsters.

'I guess I'll clear up.' It's my job, after all, as referee.

Snorri is still looking troubled. 'Bloody Spider went a bit OTT, didn't he? I mean, the newbies are expendable, but good regulars are getting hard to come by.'

'Leave it to me,' I tell him. 'I'll have a word.'

There is a small, uncomfortable pause. 'I suppose you'll want to start a new character now,' says Titania at last. 'With Philbert gone we'll need a fighter, and you've been practising, haven't you? Some of those sword moves of yours were pretty good.'

It's a touching—and a flattering—offer. There is a perceptible tension amongst my friends as I consider it, consider what it would mean. I feel a sudden affectionate burst of warmth towards them all—their familiar faces, their homemade costumes, their split-washer armour, their lines and wrinkles, their faith. But what would they do without Smithy to keep things running? It may not always be fun being a monster, but it takes commitment to do it well; commitment and a level head. Spider couldn't do it; neither could any of the others. Titania awaits my decision with a set, white face. I know how much it has cost her to suggest this; but I know my duty, too.

'I don't think so,' I tell them, shaking my head. 'I think I'd rather stick to what I'm best at.'

Within the party, the tension lessens. 'Good old Smithy,' says Veldarron, slapping my back.

'Yeah. Good old Smithy.'

I look round the circle. 'Are we on for next Saturday?'

Nods all round. 'Sure.'

'Same time, same place?'

'Might as well.'

Like I said, it has its moments. As I watch my friends walk back down the moonlit path towards the trees, I feel a complete, almost magical, sense of peace.

The enemy has been defeated, this time at least. Who knows what next week will bring? Even with my fastidious methods of waste disposal, it is unlikely that the disappearance of nine students will remain unnoticed for long. It is possible that by next Saturday—or the next—we may have to move on to new hunting grounds. Of course, it's partly the uncertainty that makes it such fun. But I do know that whatever we may face in some as-yet unimagined future, we will face it together, Veldarron, Spider, Titania and I. The regular people—with their drab, mundane, *imaginary* lives—can never understand, I realize in sudden pity; and to my surprise, I find myself beginning to whistle softly as I get out my shovel and start to dig.

Joe Hill

Joe Hill

Pop Art

Joe Hill

My best friend when I was twelve was inflatable. His name was Arthur Roth, which also made him an inflatable Hebrew, although in our now-and-then talks about the afterlife, I don't remember that he took an especially Jewish perspective. Talk was mostly what we did—in his condition rough-house was out of the question—and the subject of death, and what might follow it, came up more than once. I think Arthur knew he would be lucky to survive high school. When I met him, he had already almost been killed a dozen times, once for every year he had been alive. The afterlife was always on his mind; also the possible lack of one.

When I tell you we talked, I mean only to say we communicated, argued, put each other down, built each other up. To stick to facts, *I* talked—Art couldn't. He didn't have a mouth. When he had something to say, he wrote it down. He wore a pad around his neck on a loop of twine, and carried crayons in his pocket. He turned in school papers in crayon, took tests in crayon. You can imagine the dangers a sharpened pencil would present to a four ounce boy made of plastic and filled with air.

I think one of the reasons we were best friends was because he was such a great listener. I needed someone to listen. My mother was gone and my father I couldn't talk to. My mother ran away when I was three, sent my Dad a rambling and confused letter from Florida, about sunspots and gamma rays and the radiation that emanates from power lines, about how the birthmark on the back of her left hand had moved up her arm and onto her shoulder. After that, a couple postcards, then nothing.

As for my father, he suffered from migraines. In the afternoons, he sat in front of soaps in the darkened living room, wet-eyed and miserable. He hated to be bothered. You couldn't tell him anything. It was a mistake even to try.

'Blah blah,' he would say, cutting me off in mid-sentence. 'My head is splitting. You're killing me here with blah blah this, blah blah that.'

But Art liked to listen, and in trade, I offered him protection. Kids were scared of me. I had a bad reputation. I owned a switchblade, and sometimes I brought it to school and let other kids see; it kept them in fear. The only thing I ever stuck it into, though, was the wall of my bedroom. I'd lie on my bed and flip it at the corkboard wall, so that it hit, blade-first, *thunk!*

One day when Art was visiting he saw the pockmarks in my wall. I explained, one thing led to another, and before I knew it he was begging to have a throw.

'What's wrong with you?' I asked him. 'Is your head completely empty? Forget it. No way.'

Out came a Crayola, burnt-sienna. He wrote:

So at least let me look.

I popped it open for him. He stared at it wide-eyed. Actually, he stared at everything wide-eyed. His eyes were made of glassy plastic, stuck to the surface of his face. He couldn't blink or anything. But this was different than his usual bug-eyed stare. I could see he was really fixated.

He wrote:

I'll be careful I totally promise **please!**

I handed it to him. He pushed the point of the blade into the floor so it snicked into the handle. Then he hit the button and it snacked back out. He shuddered, stared at it in his hand. Then, without giving any warning, he chucked it at the wall. Of course it didn't hit tip-first; that takes practice, which he hadn't had, and coordination, which, speaking honestly, he wasn't ever going to have. It bounced, came flying back at him. He sprang into the air so quickly it was like I was watching his ghost jump out of his body. The knife landed where he had been and clattered away under my bed.

Pop Art

I yanked Art down off the ceiling. He wrote:

You were right, that was dumb. I'm a loser—a jerk.

'No question,' I said.
But he wasn't a loser or a jerk. My Dad is a loser. The kids at school were jerks. Art was different. He was all heart. He just wanted to be liked by someone.

Also, I can say truthfully, he was the most completely harmless person I've ever known. Not only would he not hurt a fly, he *couldn't* hurt a fly. If he slapped one, and lifted his hand, it would buzz off undisturbed. He was like a holy person in a Bible story, someone who can heal the ripped and infected parts of you with a laying-on of hands. You know how Bible stories go. That kind of person, they're never around long. Losers and jerks put nails in them and watch the air run out.

There was something special about Art, an invisible special something that just made other kids naturally want to kick his ass. He was new at our school. His parents had just moved to town. They were normal, filled with blood not air. The condition Art suffered from is one of these genetic things that plays hopscotch with the generations, like Tay-Sachs (Art told me once that he had had a grand-uncle, also inflatable, who flopped one day into a pile of leaves and burst on the tine of a buried rake). On the first day of classes, Mrs. Gannon made Art stand at the front of the room, and told everyone all about him, while he hung his head out of shyness.

He was white. Not Caucasian, *white*, like a marshmallow, or Casper. A seam ran around his head and down his sides. There was a plastic nipple under one arm, where he could be pumped with air.

Mrs. Gannon told us we had to be extra careful not to run with scissors or pens. A puncture would probably kill him. He couldn't talk; everyone had to try and be sensitive about that. His interests were astronauts, photography, and the novels of Bernard Malamud.

Before she nudged him towards his seat, she gave his shoulder an encouraging little squeeze and as she pressed her fingers into him, he whistled gently. That was the only way he ever made sound. By flexing his body he could emit little squeaks and whines. When other people squeezed him, he made a soft, musical hoot.

He bobbed down the room and took an empty seat beside me. Billy Spears, who sat directly behind him, bounced thumbtacks off his head all morning long. The first couple times Art pretended not to notice. Then, when Mrs. Gannon wasn't looking, he wrote Billy a note. It said:

> *Please stop!* I don't want to say anything to Mrs. Gannon but it isn't safe to throw thumbtacks at me. I'm not kidding.

Billy wrote back:

> You make trouble, and there won't be enough of you left to patch a tire. Think about it.

It didn't get any easier for Art from there. In biology lab, Art was paired with Cassius Delamitri, who was in sixth grade for the second time. Cassius was a fat kid, with a pudgy, sulky face, and a disagreeable film of black hair above his unhappy pucker of a mouth.

The project was to distill wood, which involved the use of a gas flame—Cassius did the work, while Art watched and wrote notes of encouragement:

> I can't believe you got a D- on this experiment when you did it last year—you totally know how to do this stuff!!

and

> My parents bought me a lab kit for my birthday. You could come over and we could play mad scientist sometime want to?

After three or four notes like that, Cassius had read enough, got it in his head Art was some kind of homosexual . . . especially with Art's talk about having him over to play doctor or whatever. When the teacher was distracted helping some other kids, Cassius shoved Art under the table and tied him around one of the table legs, in a squeaky granny knot, head, arms, body and all. When Mr. Milton asked where Art had gone, Cassius said he thought he had run to the bathroom.

'Did he?' Mr. Milton asked. 'What a relief. I didn't even know if that kid *could* go to the bathroom.'

Another time, John Erikson held Art down during recess and wrote KOLLOSTIMY BAG on his stomach with indelible marker. It was Spring before it faded away.

> The worst thing was my mom saw. Bad enough she has to know I get beat up on a daily basis. But she was really upset it was spelled wrong.

He added:

> I don't know what she expects—this is 6th grade. Doesn't she remember 6th grade? I'm sorry, but realistically, what are the odds you're going to get beat up by the grand champion of the spelling bee?

'The way your year is going,' I said. 'I figure them odds might be pretty good.'

Here is how Art and I wound up friends:

During recess periods, I always hung out at the top of the monkey bars by myself, reading sports magazines. I was cultivating my reputation as a delinquent and possible drug pusher. To help my image along, I wore a black denim jacket and didn't talk to people or make friends.

At the top of the monkey bars—a dome-shaped construction at one edge of the asphalt lot behind the school—I was a good nine feet off the ground, and had a view of the whole yard. One day I watched Billy Spears horsing around with Cassius Delamitri and John Erikson. Billy had a wiffle ball and a bat, and the three of them were trying to bat the ball in through an open second floor window. After fifteen minutes of not even coming close, John Erikson got lucky, swatted it in.

Cassius said, 'Shit—there goes the ball. We need something else to bat around.'

'Hey,' Billy shouted. 'Look! There's Art!'

They caught up to Art, who was trying to keep away, and Billy started tossing him in the air and hitting him with the bat to see how far he could knock him. Every time he struck Art with the bat it made a hollow, springy *whap!* Art popped into the air, then floated along a little ways, sinking gently back to ground. As soon as his heels touched earth he started to run, but swiftness of foot wasn't one of Art's qualities. John and Cassius got into the fun by grabbing Art and drop-kicking him, to see who could punt him highest.

The three of them gradually pummeled Art down to my end of the lot. He struggled free long enough to run in under the monkey bars. Billy caught up, struck him a whap across the ass with the bat, and shot him high into the air.

Art floated to the top of the dome. When his body touched the steel bars, he stuck, face-up—static electricity.

'Hey,' Billy hollered. 'Chuck him down here!'

I had, up until that moment, never been face to face with Art. Although we shared classes, and even sat side-by-side in Mrs. Gannon's homeroom, we had not had a single exchange. He looked at me with his enormous plastic eyes and sad blank face, and I looked right back. He found the pad around his neck, scribbled a note in spring green, ripped it off and held it up at me.

> I don't care what they do, but could you go away? I hate to get the crap knocked out of me in front of spectators.

'What's he writin'?' Billy shouted.

I looked from the note, past Art, and down at the gathering of boys below. I was struck by the sudden realization that I could *smell* them, all three of them, a damp, *human* smell, a sweaty-sour reek. It turned my stomach.

'Why are you bothering him?' I asked.

Billy said, 'Just screwin' with him.'

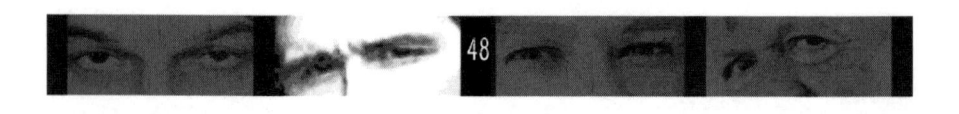

'We're trying to see how high we can make him go,' Cassius said. 'You ought to come down here. You ought to give it a try. We're going to kick him onto the roof of the friggin' school!'

'I got an even funner idea,' I said, *funner* being an excellent word to use if you want to impress on some other kids that you might be a mentally retarded psychopath. 'How about we see if I can kick your lardy ass up on the roof of the school?'

'What's your problem?' Billy asked. 'You on the rag?'

I grabbed Art and jumped down. Cassius blanched. John Erikson tottered back. I held Art under one arm, feet sticking towards them, head pointed away.

'You guys are dicks,' I said—some moments just aren't right for a funny line.

And I turned away from them. The back of my neck crawled at the thought of Billy's wiffle ball bat clubbing me one across the skull, but he didn't do a thing, let me walk.

We went out on the baseball field, sat on the pitcher's mound. Art wrote me a note that said thanks, and another that said I didn't have to do what I had done but that he was glad I had done it, and another that said he owed me one. I shoved each note into my pocket after reading it, didn't think why. That night, alone in my bedroom, I dug a wad of crushed notepaper out of my pocket, a lump the size of a lemon, peeled each note free and pressed it flat on my bed, read them all over again. There was no good reason not to throw them away, but I didn't, started a collection instead. It was like some part of me knew, even then, I might want to have something to remember Art by after he was gone. I saved hundreds of his notes over the next year, some as short as a couple words, a few six-page long manifestos. I have most of them still, from the first note he handed me, the one that begins *I don't care what they do*, to the last, the one that ends:

I want to see if it's true. If the sky opens up at the top.

At first my father didn't like Art, but after he got to know him better he really hated him.

'How come he's always mincing around?' my father asked. 'Is he a fairy or something?'

'No, Dad. He's inflatable.'

Four For Fantasy

'Well he acts like a fairy,' he said. 'You better not be queering around with him up in your room.'

Art tried to be liked—he tried to build a relationship with my father. But the things he did were misinterpreted; the statements he made were misunderstood. My Dad said something once about a movie he liked. Art wrote him a message about how the book was even better.

'He thinks I'm an illiterate,' my Dad said, as soon as Art was gone.

Another time, Art noticed the pile of worn tires heaped up behind our garage, and mentioned to my Dad about a recycling program at Sears, bring in your rotten old ones, get twenty percent off on brand-new Goodyears.

'He thinks we're trailer trash,' my Dad complained, before Art was hardly out of earshot. 'Little snotnose.'

One day Art and I got home from school, and found my father in front of the TV, with a pit bull at his feet. The bull erupted off the floor, yapping hysterically, and jumped up on Art. His paws made a slippery zipping sound sliding over Art's plastic chest. Art grabbed one of my shoulders and vaulted into the air. He could really jump when he had to. He grabbed the ceiling fan—turned off—and held on to one of the blades while the pit bull barked and hopped beneath.

'What the hell is that?' I asked.

'Family dog,' my father said. 'Just like you always wanted.'

'Not one that wants to eat my friends.'

'Get off the fan, Artie. That isn't built for you to hang off it.'

'This isn't a dog,' I said. 'It's a blender with teeth.'

'Listen, do you want to name it, or should I?' Dad asked.

Art and I hid in my bedroom and talked names.

'Snowflake,' I said. 'Sugarpie. Sunshine.'

How about Happy? That has a ring to it, doesn't it?

We were kidding, but Happy was no joke. In just a week, Art had at least three life-threatening encounters with my father's ugly dog.

If he gets his teeth in me, I'm done for. He'll punch me full of holes.

Pop Art

But Happy couldn't be housebroken, left turds scattered around the living room, hard to see in the moss brown rug. My Dad squelched through some fresh leavings once, in bare feet, and it sent him a little out of his head. He chased Happy all through the downstairs with a croquet mallet, smashed a hole in the wall, crushed some plates on the kitchen counter with a wild backswing.

The very next day, he built a chain-link pen in the sideyard. Happy went in, and that was where he stayed.

By then, though, Art was nervous to come over, and preferred to meet at his house. I didn't see the sense. It was a long walk to get to his place after school, and my house was right there, just around the corner.

'What are you worried about?' I asked him. 'He's in a pen. It's not like Happy is going to figure out how to open the door to his pen, you know.'

Art knew... but he still didn't like to come over, and when he did, he usually had a couple patches for bicycle tires on him, to guard against dark happenstance.

Once we started going to Art's every day, once it came to be a habit, I wondered why I had ever wanted us to go to my house instead. I got used to the walk—I walked the walk so many times I stopped noticing that it was long bordering on never-ending. I even looked forward to it, my afternoon stroll through coiled suburban streets, past houses done in Disney pastels: lemon, tangerine, ash. As I crossed the distance between my house and Art's house, it seemed to me that I was moving through zones of ever-deepening stillness and order, and at the walnut heart of all this peace was Art's.

Art couldn't run, talk or approach anything with a sharp edge on it, but at his house we managed to keep ourselves entertained. We watched TV. I wasn't like other kids, and didn't know anything about television. My father, I mentioned already, suffered from terrible migraines. He was home on disability, lived in the family room, and hogged our TV all day long, kept track of five different soaps. I tried not to bother him, and rarely sat down to watch with him—I sensed my presence was a distraction to him at a time when he wanted to concentrate.

Four for Fantasy

Art would have watched whatever I wanted to watch, but I didn't know what to do with a remote control. I couldn't make a choice, didn't know how. Had lost the habit. Art was a NASA buff, and we watched anything to do with space, never missed a space shuttle launch. He wrote:

> I want to be an astronaut. I'd adapt really well to being weightless. I'm **already** mostly weightless.

This was when they were putting up the international space station. They talked about how hard it was on people to spend too long in outer space. Your muscles atrophy. Your heart shrinks three sizes.

> The advantages of sending me into space keep piling up. I don't have any muscles to atrophy. I don't have any heart to shrink. I'm telling you. I'm the ideal spaceman. I belong in orbit.

'I know a guy who can help you get there. Let me give Billy Spears a call. He's got a rocket he wants to stick up your ass. I heard him talking about it.'

Art gave me a dour look, and a scribbled two word response.

Lying around Art's house in front of the tube wasn't always an option, though. His father was a piano instructor, tutored small children on the baby grand, which was in the living room along with their television. If he had a lesson, we had to find something else to do. We'd go into Art's room to play with his computer, but after twenty minutes of *row-row-row-your-boat* coming through the wall—a shrill, out-of-time plinking—we'd shoot each other sudden wild looks, and leave by way of the window, no need to talk it over.

Both Art's parents were musical, his mother a cellist. They had wanted music for Art, but it had been let-down and disappointment from the start.

> I can't even kazoo

Art wrote me once. The piano was out. Art didn't have any fingers, just a thumb, and a puffy pad where his fingers belonged. Hands like that, it had been years of work with a tutor just to learn to write legibly with a crayon. For obvious reasons, wind instruments were also out of the question; Art didn't have lungs, and didn't breathe. He tried to learn the drums, but couldn't strike hard enough to be any good at it.

His mother bought him a digital camera. 'Make music with color,' she said. 'Make melodies out of light.'

Mrs. Roth was always hitting you with lines like that. She talked about oneness, about the natural decency of trees, and she said not enough people were thankful for the smell of cut grass. Art told me when I wasn't around, she asked questions about me. She was worried I didn't have a healthy outlet for my creative self. She said I needed something to feed the inner me. She bought me a book about origami and it wasn't even my birthday.

'I didn't know the inner me was hungry,' I said to Art.

That's because it already starved to death

Art wrote.

She was alarmed to learn that I didn't have any sort of religion. My father didn't take me to church or send me to Sunday school. He said religion was a scam. Mrs. Roth was too polite to say anything to me about my father, but she said things about him to Art, and Art passed her comments on. She told Art that if my father neglected the care of my body, like he neglected the care of my spirit, he'd be in jail, and I'd be in a foster home. She also told Art that if I was put in foster care, she'd adopt me, and I could stay in the guest room. I loved her, felt my heart surge whenever she asked me if I wanted a glass of lemonade. I would have done anything she asked.

'Your Mom's an idiot,' I said to Art. 'A total moron. I hope you know that. There isn't any oneness. It's every man for himself. Anyone who thinks we're all brothers in the spirit winds up sitting under Cassius Delamitri's fat ass during recess, smelling his jock.'

Mrs. Roth wanted to take me to the synagogue—not to convert me, just as an educational experience, exposure to other cultures and all that—but Art's father shot her down, said not a chance, not our business, and what are you crazy? She had a bumper sticker on her car that showed the Star of David and the word PRIDE with a jumping exclamation point next to it.

'So Art,' I said another time. 'I got a Jewish question I want to ask you. Now you and your family, you're a bunch of hardcore Jews, right?'

> I don't know that I'd describe us as **hardcore** exactly. We're actually pretty lax. But we go to synagogue, observe the holidays—things like that.

'I thought Jews had to get their joints snipped,' I said, and grabbed my crotch. 'For the faith. Tell me—'
But Art was already writing.

> No not me. I got off. My parents were friends with a progressive Rabbi. They talked to him about it first thing after I was born. Just to find out what the official position was.

'What'd he say?'

> He said it was the official position to make an exception for anyone who would actually explode during the circumcision. They thought he was joking, but later on my Mom did some research on it. Based on what she found out, it looks like I'm in the clear—Talmudically-speaking. Mom says the foreskin has to be **skin**. If it isn't, it doesn't need to be cut.

'That's funny,' I said. 'I always thought your Mom didn't know dick. Now it turns out your Mom *does* know dick. She's an expert even. Shows what I know. Hey, if she ever wants to do more research, I have an unusual specimen for her to examine.'

And Art wrote how she would need to bring a microscope, and I said how she would need to stand back a few yards when I unzipped my pants, and back and forth, you don't need me to tell you, you can imagine the rest of the conversation for yourself. I rode Art about his mother every chance I could get, couldn't help myself. Started in on her the moment she left the room, whispering about how for an old broad she still had an okay can, and what would Art think if his father died and I married her. Art on the other hand, never once made a punch line out of my Dad. If Art ever wanted to give me a hard time, he'd make fun of how I licked my fingers after I ate, or how I didn't always wear matching socks. It isn't hard to understand why Art never stuck it to me about my father, like I stuck it to him about his mother. When your best friend is ugly—I mean bad ugly, *deformed*—you don't kid them about shattering mirrors. In a friendship, especially in a friendship between two young boys, you are allowed to inflict a certain amount of pain. This is even expected. But you must cause no serious injury; you must never, under any circumstances, leave wounds that will result in permanent scars.

Arthur's house was also where we usually settled to do our homework. In the early evening, we went into his room to study. His father was done with lessons by then, so there wasn't any plink-plink from the next room to distract us. I enjoyed studying in Art's room, responded well to the quiet, and liked working in a place where I was surrounded by books; Art had shelves and shelves of books. I liked our study time together, but mistrusted it as well. It was during our study sessions—surrounded by all that easy stillness—that Art was most likely to say something about dying.

When we talked, I always tried to control the conversation, but Art was slippery, could work death into anything.

'Some Arab *invented* the idea of the number zero,' I said. 'Isn't that weird? Someone had to think zero up.'

> Because it isn't obvious—that nothing can be something. That something which can't be measured or seen could still exist and have meaning. Same with the soul, when you think about it.

'True or false,' I said another time, when we were studying for a science quiz. 'Energy is never destroyed, it can only be changed from one form into another.'

> I hope it's true—it would be a good argument that you continue to exist after you die, even if you're transformed into something

completely different than what you had been.

He said a lot to me about death and what might follow it, but the thing I remember best was what he had to say about Mars. We were doing a presentation together, and Art had picked Mars as our subject, especially whether or not men would ever go there and try to colonize it. Art was all for colonizing Mars, cities under plastic tents, mining water from the icy poles. Art wanted to go himself.

'It's fun to imagine, maybe, fun to think about it,' I said. 'But the actual thing would be bullshit. Dust. Freezing cold. Everything red. You'd go blind looking at so much red. You wouldn't really want to do it—leave this world and never come back.'

Art stared at me for a long moment, then bowed his head, and wrote a brief note in robin's egg blue.

But I'm going to have to do that anyway. Everyone has to do that.

Then he wrote:

You get an astronaut's life whether you want it or not. Leave it all behind for a world you know nothing about. That's just the deal.

In the Spring, Art invented a game called Spy Satellite. There was a place downtown, the Party Station, where you could buy a bushel of helium-filled balloons for a quarter. I'd get a bunch, meet Art somewhere with them. He'd have his digital camera.

Soon as I handed him the balloons, he detached from the earth and lifted into the air. As he rose, the wind pushed him out and away. When he was satisfied he was high enough, he'd let go a couple balloons, level off, and start snapping pictures. When he was ready to come down, he'd just let go a few more. I'd meet him where he landed and we'd go over to his house to look at the pictures on his laptop. Photos of people swimming in their pools, men shingling their roofs;

photos of me standing in empty streets, my upturned face a miniature brown blob, my features too distant to make out; photos that always had Art's sneakers dangling into the frame at the bottom edge.

Some of his best pictures were low altitude affairs, things he snapped when he was only a few yards off the ground. Once he took three balloons and swam into the air over Happy's chain-link enclosure, off at the side of our house. Happy spent all day in his fenced-off pen, barking frantically at women going by with strollers, the jingle of the ice cream truck, squirrels. Happy had trampled all the space in his penned-in plot of earth down to mud. Scattered about him were dozens of dried piles of dogcrap. In the middle of this awful brown turdscape was Happy himself, and in every photo Art snapped of him, he was leaping up on his back legs, mouth open to show the pink cavity within, eyes fixed on Art's dangling sneakers.

I feel bad. What a horrible place to live.

'Get your head out of your ass,' I said. 'If creatures like Happy were allowed to run wild, they'd make the whole world look that way. He doesn't want to live somewhere else. Turds and mud—that's Happy's idea of a total garden spot.'

I STRONGLY disagree

Arthur wrote me, but time has not softened my opinions on this matter. It is my belief that, as a rule, creatures of Happy's ilk—I am thinking here of canines and men both—more often run free then live caged, and it is in fact a world of mud and feces they desire, a world with no Art in it, or anyone like him, a place where there is no talk of books or God or the worlds beyond this world, a place where the only communication is the hysterical barking of starving and hate-filled dogs.

One Saturday morning, mid-April, my Dad pushed the bedroom door open, and woke me up by throwing my sneakers on my bed. 'You have to be at the dentist's in half an hour. Put your rear in gear.'

I walked—it was only a few blocks—and I had been sitting in the waiting room for twenty minutes, dazed with boredom, when I remembered I had told Art that I'd be coming by his house as soon as I got up. The receptionist let me use the phone to call him.

His mom answered. 'He just left to see if he could find you at your house,' she told me.

I called my Dad.

'He hasn't been by,' he said. 'I haven't seen him.'

'Keep an eye out.'

'Yeah well. I've got a headache. Art knows how to use the doorbell.'

I sat in the dentist's chair, my mouth stretched open and tasting of blood and mint, and struggled with unease and an impatience to be going. Did not perhaps trust my father to be decent to Art without myself present. The dentist's assistant kept touching my shoulder and telling me to relax.

When I was all through and got outside, the deep and vivid blueness of the sky was a little disorientating. The sunshine was headache-bright, bothered my eyes. I had been up for two hours, still felt cotton-headed and dull-edged, not all the way awake. I jogged.

The first thing I saw, standing on the sidewalk, was Happy, free from his pen. He didn't so much as bark at me. He was on his belly in the grass, head between his paws. He lifted sleepy eyelids to watch me approach, then let them sag shut again. His pen door stood open in the side yard.

I was looking to see if he was lying on a heap of tattered plastic when I heard the first feeble tapping sound. I turned my head and saw Art in the back of my father's station wagon, smacking his hands on the window. I walked over and opened the door. At that instant, Happy exploded from the grass with a peal of mindless barking. I grabbed Art in both arms, spun and fled. Happy's teeth closed on a piece of my flapping pantleg. I heard a tacky ripping sound, stumbled, kept going.

I ran until there was a stitch in my side and no dog in sight—six blocks, at least. Toppled over in someone's yard. My pantleg was sliced open from the back of my knee to the ankle. I took my first good look at Art. It was a jarring sight. I was so out of breath, I could only produce a thin, dismayed little squeak—the sort of sound Art was always making.

Pop Art

His body had lost its marshmallow whiteness. It had a gold-brown duskiness to it now, so it resembled a marshmallow, lightly toasted. He seemed to have deflated to about half his usual size. His chin sagged into his body. He couldn't hold his head up.

Art had been crossing our front lawn, when Happy burst from his hiding place under one of the hedges. In that first crucial moment, Art saw he would never be able to outrun our family dog on foot. All such an effort would get him would be an ass full of fatal puncture wounds. So instead, he jumped into the station wagon, and slammed the door.

The windows were automatic—there was no way to roll them down. Any door he opened, Happy tried to jam his snout in at him. It was seventy degrees outside the car, over a hundred inside. Art watched in dismay as Happy flopped in the grass beside the wagon to wait.

Art sat. Happy didn't move. Lawnmowers droned in the distance. The afternoon passed. In time Art began to wilt in the heat. He became ill and groggy. His plastic skin started sticking to the seats.

Then you showed up. Just in time. You saved my life.

But my eyes blurred and tears dripped off my face onto his note. I hadn't come just in time—not at all.

Art was never the same. His skin stayed a filmy yellow, and he developed a deflation problem. His parents would pump him up, and for a while he'd be all right, his body swollen with oxygen, but eventually he'd go saggy and limp again. His doctor took one look and told his parents not to put off the trip to Disney World another year.

I wasn't the same either. I was miserable—couldn't eat, suffered unexpected stomachaches, brooded and sulked.

'Wipe that look off your face,' my father said one night at dinner. 'Life goes on. Deal with it.'

I was dealing all right. I knew the door to Happy's pen didn't open itself. I punched holes in the tires of the station wagon, then left my switchblade sticking out of one of them, so my father would know for sure who had done it. He had police officers come over and pretend to arrest me. They drove me around in the squad car and talked tough at me for a while, then said they'd bring me home if I'd 'get with the program.' The next day I locked Happy in the wagon and he took a shit on the driver's seat. My father collected all the books Art had got me to read, the Bernard Malamud, the Ray Bradbury, the Isaac Bashevis Singer. He burned them on the barbecue grill.

'How do you feel about that, smart guy?' He asked me, while he squirted lighter fluid on them.

'Okay with me,' I said. 'They were on your library card.'

That summer, I spent a lot of time sleeping over at Art's.

Don't be angry. No one is to blame.

Art wrote me.

'Get your head out of your ass,' I said, but then I couldn't say anything else because it made me cry just to look at him.

Late August, Art gave me a call. It was a hilly four miles to Scarswell Cove, where he wanted us to meet, but by then months of hoofing it to Art's after school had hardened me to long walks. I had plenty of balloons with me, just like he asked.

Scarswell Cove is a sheltered, pebbly beach on the sea, where people go to stand in the tide and fish in waders. There was no one there except a couple old fishermen, and Art, sitting on the slope of the beach. His body looked soft and saggy, and his head lolled forward, bobbled weakly on his non-existent neck. I sat down beside him. Half a mile out, the dark blue waves were churning up icy combers.

'What's going on?' I asked.

Art bowed his head. He thought a bit. Then he began to write.

He wrote:

*Do you know people have made it into outer space without rockets? Chuck Yeagher flew a high performance jet so high it started to tumble—it tumbled **upwards**, not downwards. He ran*

> so high, gravity lost hold of him. His jet was tumbling up out of the stratosphere. All the color melted out of the sky. It was like the blue sky was paper, and a hole was burning out the middle of it, and behind it, everything was black. Everything was full of stars. Imagine falling **UP**.

I looked at this note, then back to his face. He was writing again. His second message was simpler.

> I've had it. Seriously—I'm all done. I deflate 15—16 times a day. I need someone to pump me up practically every hour. I feel sick all the time and I hate it. This is no kind of life.

'Oh no,' I said. My vision blurred. Tears welled up and spilled over my eyes. 'Things will get better.'

> No. I don't think so. It isn't about whether I die. It's about figuring out where. And I've decided. I'm going to see how high I can go. I want to see if it's true. If the sky opens up at the top.

I don't know what else I said to him. A lot of things, I guess. I asked him not to do it, not to leave me. I said that it wasn't fair. I said that I didn't have any other friends. I said that I had always been lonely. I talked until it was all blubber and strangled, helpless sobs, and he reached his crinkly plastic arms around me and held me while I hid my face in his chest.

He took the balloons from me, got them looped around one wrist. I held his other hand and we walked to the edge of the water. The surf splashed in and filled my sneakers. The sea was so cold it made the bones in my feet throb. I lifted him and held him in both arms, and squeezed until he made a mournful squeak. We hugged for a long time. Then I opened my arms. I let him go. I hope if there is another world, we will not be judged too harshly for the things we did wrong here—that we will at least be forgiven for the mistakes we made out of love. I have no doubt it was a sin of some kind, to let such a one go.

He rose away and the airstream turned him around so he was looking back at me as he bobbed out over the water, his left arm pulled high over his head, the balloons attached to his wrist. His head was tipped at a thoughtful angle, so he seemed to be studying me.

I sat on the beach and watched him go. I watched until I could no longer distinguish him from the gulls that were wheeling and diving over the water, a few miles away. He was just one more dirty speck wandering the sky. I didn't move. I wasn't sure I could get up. In time, the horizon turned a dusky rose and the blue sky above deepened to black. I stretched out on the beach, and watched the stars spill through the darkness overhead. I watched until a dizziness overcame me, and I could imagine spilling off the ground, and falling up into the night.

I developed emotional problems. When school started again, I would cry at the sight of an empty desk. I couldn't answer questions or do homework. I flunked out and had to go through seventh grade again.

Worse, no one believed I was dangerous anymore. It was impossible to be scared of me after you had seen me sobbing my guts out a few times. I didn't have the switchblade anymore; my father had confiscated it.

Billy Spears beat me up one day, after school—mashed my lips, loosened a tooth. John Erikson held me down, wrote COLLISTAMY BAG on my forehead in magic marker. Still trying to get it right. Cassius Delamitri ambushed me, shoved me down and jumped on top of me, crushing me under his weight, driving all the air out of my lungs. A defeat by way of deflation; Art would have understood perfectly.

I avoided the Roths'. I wanted more than anything to see Art's mother, but stayed away. I was afraid if I talked to her, it would come pouring out of me, that I had been there at the end, that I stood in the surf and let Art go. I was afraid of what I might see in her eyes; of her hurt and anger.

Less than six months after Art's deflated body was found slopping in the surf along North Scarswell beach, there was a FOR SALE sign out in front of the Roth's ranch. I never saw either of his parents again. Mrs. Roth sometimes wrote me letters, asking how I was and what I was doing, but I never replied. She signed her letters *love*.

I went out for track in high school, and did well at pole vault. My track coach said the law of gravity didn't apply to me. My track coach didn't know fuckall about gravity. No matter how high I went for a moment, I always came down in the end, same as anyone else.

Pole vault got me a state college scholarship. I kept to myself. No one at college knew me, and I was at last able to rebuild my long lost image as a sociopath. I didn't go to parties. I didn't date. I didn't want to get to know anybody.

I was crossing the campus one morning, and I saw coming towards me a young girl, with black hair so dark it had the cold blue sheen of rich oil. She wore a bulky sweater and a librarian's ankle-length skirt; a very asexual outfit, but all the same you could see she had a stunning figure, slim hips, high ripe breasts. Her eyes were of staring blue glass, her skin as white as Art's. It was the first time I had seen an inflatable person since Art drifted away on his balloons. A kid walking behind me wolf-whistled at her. I stepped aside, and when he went past, I tripped him up and watched his books fly everywhere.

'Are you some kind of psycho?' he screeched.

'Yes,' I said. 'Exactly.'

Her name was Ruth Goldman. She had a round rubber patch on the heel of one foot where she had stepped on a shard of broken glass as a little girl, and a larger square patch on her left shoulder where a sharp branch had poked her once on a windy day. Home schooling and obsessively protective parents had saved her from further damage. We were both English majors. Her favorite writer was Kafka—because he understood the absurd. My favorite writer was Malamud—because he understood loneliness.

We married the same year I graduated. Although I remain doubtful about the life eternal, I converted without any prodding from her, gave in at last to a longing to have some talk of the spirit in my life. Can you really call it a conversion? In truth, I had no beliefs to convert from. Whatever the case, ours was a Jewish wedding, glass under white cloth, crunched beneath the bootheel.

One afternoon I told her about Art.

That's so sad. I'm so sorry.

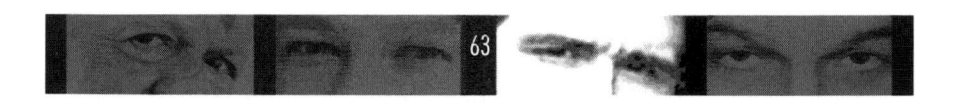

Four For Fantasy

She wrote to me in wax pencil. She put her hand over mine.

What happened? Did he run out of air?

'Ran out of sky,' I said.

Richard Christian Matheson

Richard Christian Matheson

City of Dreams

Richard Christian Matheson

It was June when the Royal moved in.

I knew because high, metal fences started going up, perimeter shrubbery doubled, and two sullen Dobermans began patrolling. Then, overnight, an intercom, numerical keypad and security camera were mysteriously installed, at the bottom of the Royal's driveway, which ran alongside mine. Whenever I drove by, the lens would zoom to inspect me, staring with curt inquisition.

The Royal was obviously concerned who visited.

Had the Royal been hurt? Was future hurt likely? Were death threats being phoned in hourly? It seemed anything, however dire, was possible. I was already feeling badly for the Royal.

I didn't know if the Royal was a him or her. Rock diva? Zillionaire cyber tot? Mob boss? Pro-leaguer? My mind wandered in lush possibility.

But all I ever saw was a moody limo that purred through the gate and crunched up the long driveway. By the time it got to the big house, the forest landscaping hid it; a leafy moat. I found it all rather troubling. In my experience, concealment is meaningful; trees can be trimmed, the fears which lurk behind them are a different story. Ultimately, one cannot hide, only camouflage. Orson Welles certainly understood this; in *Citizen Kane,* tragic privilege never seemed so rapturous, nor incarcerated.

As days passed, I tried not to listen to what went on next door. I'd play jazz CDs, sip morning espresso, scan the entertainment section for reviews, to distract my attentions. But my community is exclusive and quiet, and bird's wings, as they groom, are noticeable. It made it hard to miss the Royal's limo as it sighed up the driveway, obscured by the half million dollars of pre-meditated forest.

Once parked, doors would open and close, and I'd hear footsteps, sometimes cheerless murmurs; the limo driver speaking to the Royal, I assumed. Russian? Indo-Chinese? Impossible to tell. Then, the front door to the house would slam with imperial finality.

It went on like that for two weeks.

I began to think, perhaps, I should be a better neighbor, make the Royal feel more welcome; a part of the local family. Which is somewhat misleading considering the neighborhood is an aloof haven and I barely know anyone. I'm like that; keep to myself, make friends slowly. I'm what they call an observer. Some dive, I float with mask and snorkel. But the instinct seemed warm; welcoming.

I was also getting very curious.

I was up late writing, one night, and decided to mix-up a batch of chocolate chip cookies. My new screenplay was coming along well, if slowly, and I thought about love scenes and action scenes as I peered into the oven, watching the huge cookies rise like primitive islands forming. They were plump, engorged with cubes of chocolate the size of small dice; worthy of a Royal, I decided.

I let them cool, ate three, wrapped the remaining dozen in tin-foil. Crumpled the foil to make it resemble something snappy and Audubon, the way they make crinkly swans in nice places to shroud left-overs. I wrapped a bow around the neck, placed the tin-foil bird into a pretty box I'd saved from Christmas, ribboned it, found a greeting card with no message. The photo on the front was a natural cloud formation that looked a bit like George Lucas.

I used my silver-ink pen that flows upside down, like something a doomed astronaut might use to write a final entry, and wrote 'Some supplies to keep you happy and safe. Researchers say chocolate brings on the exact sensation of love; an effect of phenolamine. (Just showing off). Welcome to this part of the world.'

My P.S. was a phone number, at the house, in case the Royal ever 'needed anything.' I also included a VHS of François Truffaut's *Day For Night,* a film I especially love for its tipsy discernment.

I debated whether to include any exclamation marks, thought it excess, opted for periods. Clean, emotionally stable. Friendly but not cloying. Being in the film business, I knew first impressions counted.

It's one reason I'm sought after to do scripts, albeit for lesser films with sinking talents. But I'm well paid and it allows me to live in this secured community near L.A., complete with gate-guard, acre parcels and compulsory privacy. I'm an anonymous somebody; primarily rumor. I wish I could've been Faulkner, but there you are. I'm a faceless credit on a screen; my scant reply to a world's indifference.

I left the cookies and card in the Royal's mail-box, at the bottom of the driveway, and spoke tense baby-talk to the Dobermans, as I made the deposit, like one of those pocked thugs in *The French Connection*. The package fit nicely, looked cheerful in there. Too much so? I considered it. Every detail determines outcome; it's the essence of subtext, as Frank Capra once observed. And certainly, if the Royal were truly an international sort, I wanted there to be room for some kind of friendship. I could learn things. Get gossip that mattered; the chic lowdown.

I waited two days. A week.

Nothing.

I'd sit by my pool, every morning, read the paper, scan box-office numbers, sip espresso. But I wasn't paying full attention. I was watching my Submariner tick.

At ten-thirty, sharp, the heavy tires would crunch up the driveway and the door ritual would begin. I couldn't make out a word and tried to remember if I'd left my phone number in the P.S. Even if not, there was always my mailbox. Concern was devouring me by ounces and I disliked seeing it happen.

In self protection, I began to lose interest in the Royal; the inky sleigh, the seeming apathy, the whole damn thing.

At least that's what I tried to tell myself.

Sergio Leone says the important thing about film making is to make a world that is 'not now.' A *real* world, a *genuine* world, but one that allows myth its vital seepage. Sergio contends that myth is everything. I suppose one could take that too far.

Two weeks passed quickly and I'd heard nothing. I felt deflated, yet oddly exhilarated to be snubbed by someone so important; it bordered on eerie intoxicant, even hinted at voodoo. Despite efforts otherwise, the truth was I continued to wonder what the Royal thought about me, though it hardly constituted preoccupation.

I'm a bit sensitive on the topic because my ex-wife often said I paid unnatural attention to those I considered remarkable, though I found nothing strange in such focus. The way I see it, we all need heroes; dreams of something better; perhaps even transcendent. A key piece of miscellany: she ran off with a famous hockey player from Ketchikan, Alaska; a slab of idiocy named Stu. TIME and NEWSWEEK covered their nuptials. Color photos, confetti, the whole bit. A featured quote from her gushed:

'I've never been happier!'

Real pain. Like I'd been shot.

I feel it places things, as regards my outlook, in perspective. She certainly never could. Strangely enough, I've been thinking about her lately; how she drove me into psychotherapy after she left and took our African Grey, Norman, with her and never contacted me again, saying I'd made them both miserable. Over time, I heard from mutual friends that she was claiming, among other toxic side effects of our marriage, that I'd caused Norman to stop talking, and that once they'd set-up house elsewhere, he became a chatterbox. I took it personally; couldn't sleep for weeks.

More haunting facts of my teetering world.

The fate of the cookies preyed on my mind for days, affecting work and sleep, a predicament rife with what my ex-shrink, Larry, used to term 'emotional viscosity,' a condition I suspect he made-up, hoping it would catch on and bring him, and his unnerving beard, acclaim. Still, I wrote half-heartedly and my stomach churned the kind of butter that really clogs you up.

Another few days went by and I made no move. Any choice seemed wrong; quietude the only wisdom. I was feeling foolish; mocked. My heartfelt efforts had been more irrelevant than I'd feared. I continued to work on my screenplay, and joked emptily with my agent, who seemed an especially drab series of noises compared to the person I knew the Royal must be.

It's true, I had no real evidence. The Royal might be an overwhelming bore. Some rich cadaver in an iron lung, staring bitterly into a tiny mirror.

But I didn't think so.

In fact, I was beginning to think anyone who went to such trouble to avoid a friendly overture had something precious to protect. On a purely personal level, if cookies, a card and a badly executed foil swan could scare a person, their levels of sensitivity had to be finely calibrated. Perhaps the Royal had been wounded; given up on humanity. I've been there. I wish somebody like me tried to crack the safe; get me the hell out.

But when's the last time life had a heart. Let's face it, unsoothed by human kindness, souls recede. It's in all the great movies; pain, sacrifice, hopes in dissolution.

It's how people like me and the Royal got the way we are. We flee emotionally, too riddled by personal travail to venture human connection. Sort of like Norman. We're just recovering believers, choking on the soot of an angry world.

I understood the Royal. Yet I had to move on; get over it.

But it was hard. Maybe I was simply in some futile trance, succumbed to loneliness and curiosity. I admit I'm easily infected by my enthusiasms. You read about people like me; the ones who do something crazy in the name of human decency only to find themselves stuffed, hung on a wall; poached by life.

So, despite rejection, I found myself listening each morning, over breakfast, to the Royal's property, gripped by speculation. Awaiting the door ritual, sensing the Royal over there, alone, needing a friend. It was sad and nearly called out for a melancholic soundtrack; something with strings; that haunted Bernard Herrmann ambivalence.

It made me recall a line I once heard in a bleak, Fassbinder movie; this Munich prostitute whispered to her lover that a person's fate 'always escorts the bitter truth.' She blew Gitane smoke, pouting with succulent blankness and, to my embarrassment, it just spoke to me. I don't know why. It got me thinking, I suppose, the ways movies can; even the sorry, transparent ones.

It was the first time I began to consciously wish I could do a second draft of me, start things over; find my life a more worthy plot, tweak the main character. Maybe even find a theme. A man without one has nowhere to hide.

Ingmar Bergman based a career on it.

T wo days later, the note came.

In my mailbox, dozing in an expensive, ragcloth envelope. It was handwritten, the letters a sensual perfection.

We must meet. How about drinks tonight over here. Around sunset?

I must have read it a hundred times, weighing each word, the phrasing and inclusion of the word 'must'. It seemed not without meaning.

I debated outfits. Formal? Casual? I was able to make a case for either, chose slacks, a sweater. I looked nice; thought it important.

Before heading over, I considered a gift. Cheese? An unopened compact disc? Mahler? Coltraine? But it strained of effort and I wanted to seem offhand; worth knowing. The way Jimmy Stewart always was; presuming nothing, evincing worlds.

I used the forgotten path between the two driveways, dodging the dobermans, who seemed to expect me, tilting heads with professional interest, beady-eyes ashimmer.

I walked to the front door. Knocked. Waited two minutes, listened for footsteps, and was about to knock, again, when the door opened.

She was *exquisite*.

Maybe twenty. Eyes and dress mystic blue, dark hair, medium length. Skin, countess-pale. She wore a platinum locket, and gauged me for a moment.

'Hello,' she said, in the best voice I've ever heard, up till then, or since.

We spent an hour talking about everything, though I learned little about her. At some point, she said her name was Aubrey and I'm sure I responded, though I was lost in her smile, her attentions colorizing my world.

It seemed she told me less about herself with each passing minute, which I liked; she was obviously the real thing. Genuine modesty looks best on the genuinely important.

She asked me about my work and carefully listened as I spoke about why I loved the music of words and the fantasy of movies; of creating perfect impossibilities. Her rare features silhouetted on mimosa sunset, and she said she'd always loved films, especially romantic ones, and when her smile took my heart at gunpoint, I felt swept into a costly special effect, a trick of film and moment, as if part of a movie in which I'd been terribly miscast; my presence too common to properly elevate the material.

She took my hand, and when we walked outside and watched stars daisy the big pool, I thought I must be falling in love. I still think I was, despite everything soon to befall me.

After a slow walk around her fountained garden, she said she was tired and needed her rest, that she' d come a very long way. I wish I'd thought to ask for details of that journey; an oversight which torments me to this second.

Aubrey slowly slipped her delicate hands around my waist and it almost seemed like loss had found us; a moment nearly cinematic in composition.

She said she had a gift for me, and led me to a wrapped package that rest, on a chaise, near the pool.

'I made it,' she said.

'A painting?' I guessed, reaching to open it, until she gently stopped me.

'Tomorrow,' she suggested. 'When you're alone.'

It seemed she was being dramatic. I wish it had been anywhere near that simple.

'Goodnight.' Her full lips uncaged the word, as she looked up into my eyes, vulnerably.

I protested, wanting to know more about her, but she placed her mouth to my ear.

'I've always looked for you out there,' she said, softly, voice a despairing melody. 'In the dark. I've wondered what you were like.'

'What do you mean?' I finally replied, lost.

She never answered and I watched her disappear into the mansion, with a final wave, and what I would describe, in a script, if I had to tell the actress what to convey, as veiled desperation.

The next morning, I slept so deeply I didn't even hear the car that sped up my driveway. It wasn't until the knocking that I finally awakened.

When the detective spoke, I felt the earth die.

'A break-in?' I repeated in a voice that had to sound in need of medical attention.

He explained the missing piece was valuable, purchased in London, at auction. The chaffeur had told the police the owner of the house was a collector, but gave no further details.

'It was a gift. She gave it to me,' I explained.

'She?'

'Aubrey.' I could still see her plaintive eyes, desperate for connection. 'The woman who lives there.'

He said nothing.

Asked if he could see it.

I nodded and took him to my living room, where it leaned against the big sofa. He slowly, silently, unwrapped it and my world began to vanish.

The poster was full color, gold-framed.

It was from the thirties and the star was a stunning brute named Dan Drake; unshaven and clefted. His beautiful co-star was Isabella Ryan, and she was held in his embrace as the two stood atop Mulholland Drive, windblown; somehow doomed. Behind them, a stoic L.A. glittered, morose precincts starved of meaning. Though striking, no splendor could be found in its image, merely loss. The movie was titled *City of Dreams,* but I'd never heard of it.

Isabella's eyes and dress were mystic blue, her flowing dark hair and pale skin more regal than the platinum locket adorning her slender neck.

From any angle, no matter how inaccurately observed, she not only resembled Aubrey, she was her.

It was shocking to me in a way I'd never experienced and I nearly felt some cruel director zooming onto my numbed expression for the telling close-up.

Both stars had signed at the bottom.

'To everyone who ever loved. Yours, Dan Drake'

Beside his, in delicate script was:

'I've always seen you out there. You're in my dreams. Love, Isabella Ryan'

She seemed to be looking right at me, disguising a profound fear.

Charges were never brought against me, and the sunken-faced detective said I'd gotten off easy, that my neighbor, still unnamed, didn't want trouble and was giving me a second chance. The Royal only wanted the poster back, nothing more. For me, this generosity stirred further mystique; intolerable distress.

It's futile to determine who I'd actually spent the evening with; I don't believe in ghosts unless they are of the emotional variety; aroused by seances of personal misfortune, you might say.

But this thought brings no peace, no clarity.

I looked up *City of Dreams* in one of my movie books and found it; 1942, MGM. Black and white. Suspense. 123 minutes. There was a related article about Isabella, an air-brushed studio photo beside her husband, the obscure composer Malcolm Zinner. Zinner was bespeckled, intense. It appeared their marriage had been loveless.

The book said she'd had a nervous breakdown, but then don't they all? She'd never done another movie after *City of Dreams,* despite promising reviews, and died in a plane crash, in 1953. The book said her real name was Aubrey Baker.

Truffaut said that film is truth, twenty-four frames per second. Mine seems to be moving rather slower these days, my heart circling itself. I feel drenched by confusion; a lost narrative. I am drawn to unhealthy theory and wonder if perhaps I am dying.

Maybe I've just seen too many movies.

My ex-wife used to say the thing about irony is you never see it coming; that's how you know it's there. Also, the bigger it is, the more its invisibility and caprice. She used to talk like that, in puzzles. I'm not sure what she was getting at, but there you are.

All I know, is a movie poster with a long dead beauty, had been the most genuine thing I could remember in a lifetime of misappropriated and badly written fictions; it seemed a bad trend. Not even a particularly worthwhile plot, but I was never much good at that part.

Meanwhile, the Royal, it appears, is out there somewhere, hidden by lawyers; filtered and untouched. Bereft, bled by abuse and event; disfigurations of neglect.

It's been two months now, since that evening by the pool, and still no sign of the Royal, who remains at large in elite silence. I suppose I've given up thinking we'll ever actually meet, barring the extreme twist.

Sometimes, I find myself staring at the handwritten invitation, which I saved, though I have no idea who really wrote it. I stare until the words lift from the paper and fly away, scattering grammar into sky; an image Vittorio De Sica might have sparked to.

Four for Fantasy

After considerable search, I finally found a copy of *City of Dreams* at a specialty video store, which had to track it down for me. When I watch Aubrey, despite her astonishing beauty, I keep thinking she looks trapped; not by bad dialogue or plot, but an apprehension of her life to be. Its imminent ruin.

Today, I tried to tell my agent why the dumb script I've been working on is late, and when he heard all of what had happened, he sighed and said writers were always getting themselves in crazy messes. He said he thought I'd probably seen Isabella's movie when I was a kid and forgotten about it.

He nearly accused me of drinking, again, and wondered if maybe I'd had too much one night, wandered around the Royal's house and seen the poster; decided I had to have it, succumbing to stupid nostalgia. To bring back my only good childhood memory; going to the movies. The rest had been loveless, terrifying; an ordeal that lasted for endless seasons of pain.

I'm sure he's right. I do drink when I get lonely. I could take many evenings out of your life failing to convey the dread and hurt I often feel. I've had nights where I stared pointlessly, out at the world, and thought that no one could ever love me, just as, it seems, Isabella watches it from her lurid, heartbreaking poster, searching for the one face out there, in a heartless city, who will truly care.

Bunuel said every life is a film. Some good, some bad. We are, each of us, paradoxes in an unstated script; pawns who wish to know kings, souls divided, hearts in exile. We're all tragic characters, one way or the other; the vivid Technicolor glories, the noir hurts, the dissolve to final credits.

Fellini believed movies were magic, itself, awakened by light. That theaters were churches, dim and velvet; filled with incantation.

All I know is that when you feel lost and wounded, movies always welcome you, like a friend, inviting you to forget the painful truth; embracing your most lightless fragilities, the sadnesses which bind you.

To dream of better things.

Life pales.